Dare To Be Different
with ROBYN BURNETT

ECW PRESS

Copyright © Quincy Mack Entertainment Inc., 2002

Published by ECW PRESS
2120 Queen Street East, Suite 200, Toronto, Ontario, Canada M4E 1E2

All rights reserved. No part of this publication may be reproduced, stored in a retrieval system, or transmitted in any form by any process — electronic, mechanical, photocopying, recording, or otherwise — without the prior written permission of the copyright owners and ECW PRESS.

NATIONAL LIBRARY OF CANADA CATALOGUING IN PUBLICATION DATA

Mack, Quincy
Q Mack: dare to be different / Quincy Mack
ISBN 1-55022-572-3

1. Children — Conduct of life. 2. Teenagers — Conduct of life. I. Title
LB1065.M32 2003   158.1´083   C2002-905433-8

Cover and Text Design and Typesetting: Tania Craan
Front cover photo: Erin Riley
Printing: Transcontinental

The publication of *Q Mack* has been generously supported by the Canada Council, the Ontario Arts Council, and the Government of Canada through the Book Publishing Industry Development Program. Canadä

DISTRIBUTION
CANADA: Jaguar Book Group, 100 Armstrong Avenue, Georgetown, ON, L7G 5S4

UNITED STATES: Independent Publishers Group, 814 North Franklin Street, Chicago, Illinois 60610

PRINTED AND BOUND IN CANADA

ECW PRESS
ecwpress.com

Contents

1. **Basketball Tryouts with Wally and The Undertaker**   *1*
2. **The Sleeping Bag**   *11*
3. **Saturday Morning Madness**   *19*
4. **It Could Be Worse**   *29*
5. **Michael Jordan's Losing Streak**   *41*
6. **Johnny, the Ladies, and the Trip to McDonald's**   *47*
7. **Major Influencer??**   *57*

8 *There's No Such Thing as a Perfect Player* **67**

9 *M.J. and The Great One* **83**

10 *The Correct Formula* **107**

"It's Showtime, Baby!" **131**

The Little Known FAQ **145**

Basketball Tryouts with Wally and The Undertaker

In grade 10, I went to try out for the junior basketball team. The coaches, Doug Aitchison and his assistant Wally Schlithorn, were absolute basketball freaks. These guys loved basketball and still do. They were coaching the junior team, basically the 15/16-year-old boys at the high school. For the tryouts, these guys decided to take a new approach.

"You know what?" they thought. "We want to see what kind of choices these guys are going to make this year. We want to see before we even pick a team."

Q Mack

The first thing they did was set the first practice at 5:45 a.m. That is before six o'clock in the morning ... on a school day! In Canada, as with the NBA, high school basketball begins November first. So our practices also started in the beginning of November. Now in Canada, and in Brantford especially, at this point in the year, snow is a 50/50 possibility. And as you get into December, you know there are going to be all kinds of mornings where you have to walk to school outside. And if you're walking to school at 5:15 or 5:30 in the morning you're going to be walking in the dark *and* in the snow. Doug and Wally knew that by placing the practice at a crazy time in the morning, they weren't really going to choose the team, the team was going to choose itself. And on that morning, about 45 to 48 dudes came out for the junior basketball team tryouts. This was day number one.

Forty-five guys stood in the gym that morning, at 5:45 a.m. The lights were just coming on. It was still cold in the gym and it couldn't have been more than two or three degrees Celsius outside. We all stood in that gym and thought, "Well, at least this is going to be a new experience. We're gonna be playing

Basketball Tryouts with Wally and The Undertaker

basketball, shooting some hoops, early in the morning. . . . This will be great!"

But Wally and Doug had different plans.

Wally and Doug decided there would be absolutely no basketball playing on day number one. We thought this was insane. We thought, "What do you mean there'll be no basketball playing?"

"Oh, we're gonna run a lot of drills, and we're gonna do a lot of different skills, and definitely have a little bit of talk time, a little chalk talk as well, but we won't need any basketballs for today," they told us.

And we all kind of thought, "Well that's weird, but we'll go with the flow. We don't have any choice." But we always did have a choice.

Coach Doug Aitchison stands about six foot six and at the time weighed about 245 pounds. He resembled "The Undertaker" from the WWF: the old World Wrestling Federation. In fact, he even played "The Undertaker" in a lot of the school "Wrestle-Ramas" that we put on for charity or to raise money for different school teams. To have our junior coach, who was all serious and basketball-minded, letting loose and playing a role in front of the entire school

> Q Mack

was a lot of fun for the team. And because we knew that he would "sell out" and do this as a way of raising some money for our team, we knew we had to "sell out" for him and really pay attention in practice and listen to what was going on.

So, back to day number one. All we did was run. From 5:50 in the morning 'til 6:30, it was pure running. Three lines of dudes in groups of fifteen on the end line had to run down to the free-throw line, touch it, then run back to the end line. Over and over. Then, it moved to the half-court line. Run and touch that line. Then all the way back to the starting point. These are called wind-sprints. Our coaches referred to them as the "Texas Ironman." We ran wind-sprints for about 45 minutes. After awhile, there were people being physically sick to their stomachs in the washroom, or running over to garbage cans. People were leaving in the middle of practice saying, "If we're not gonna get basketballs out, I'm outta here!" All of a sudden I saw four or five guys go to the locker room, claiming they were sick and then they stayed in the locker room. Now our practice was down to 41 hopeful junior basketball players.

Basketball Tryouts with Wally and The Undertaker

As 6:35 came we thought, "Well we're gonna have to get some basketballs out now to do some lay-ups."

"No no. No balls yet. What we're going to do now is work on some defensive drills."

Defensive stance is a similar position to sitting on a low stool. You get a real sweet feelin' in the hamstrings and quads after being in this position for a couple of minutes. But it's not just striking that stance: it's sliding left to right, touching lines while *in* that stance. And whenever you hear "HIT THE DECK," that means, "Touch your chest on the ground and jump back onto your feet as soon as possible." If you heard "Machine Gun Funk," it meant crazy feet. "Crazy feet" is almost like running on the spot, triple time but down in the defensive stance. So this went on for the next 30 minutes.

During this time, we had about 16 people walk out of the gym saying, "I've had enough of this. I'm outta here. This is ridiculous." Now our practice crew was down to about 25. At about 6:55 a.m. we thought, "Well finally. We're tired, you know, we're totally out of breath. We've been running for about an hour and fifteen minutes straight. Time to get the basketballs out. Yes. Here we go!"

Q Mack

Well, not so fast. The coaches had a different idea. First they started to talk about a drill that required the basketballs . . . and yet, suddenly we're expected to run full court lay-up shots to work on the footwork but with *no basketballs*. As soon as the 25 remaining hopefuls heard we were going to be running full court lay-ups with no basketballs, we thought, "What, are you kidding me? This is ridiculous." Without even sticking around to find out, out went another seven people.

What the coaches wanted to look at wasn't just footwork, but coach-ability. They wanted to see who was willing to do what it takes to be part of a cohesive, well-oiled unit. They were testing the waters to see what choices in attitude people would make. And some people chose to leave that gym that day while others chose to stay. Now we had about 18 kids standing in that gym. The coach called everybody in and said,

"This team is beginning to choose itself."

At that time, everybody looked at everyone else and thought "Hmmm. We're all here by choice right now." It was 7:15, and the vibe of the eye contact between every player there was, "We're all here by choice. We're all going to be here no matter what the obstacle is. We're gonna be here toughing this out and we're going to be the ones to decide if we want to be on this team or not."

The next day all 18 kids came back, and by day number three, the coaches were able to cut the basketball squad down to the 12 players that they wanted to run with that year. The other six players who had stuck it out but been cut were always invited to gym time, even practice time. They were always welcome to come in and work on their skills, because they showed the heart. They made the choice to have a positive attitude and to be "coachable."

The stage that you find yourself in life is directly created — directly molded — by the choices that you make and the attitude that you take. The situations you're going to find yourself in are because of choices that you made earlier that day, earlier that week, earlier that year.

Choices create the world that we live in. We create this world with every thought that we think, with every word that we speak, and with every action that we take. Now that's a lot to grasp, a lot to think about

Q Mack

right there. I think it's important to realize that very early in life, the choices that you make will create your world as you know it. Whatever your reality is, 99% of the time it comes from the choices that you make. If you think back to any situation you've found yourself in — a sticky situation, a rough time that you've gone through, a happy time that you've had, how you ended up where you were on a particular day or how you succeeded or failed — you found yourself laughing or crying because of a choice that you made at some point. The biggest choice that anybody ever has is always the *choice of attitude.* The best part is, you always have a choice when it comes to attitude. If you're put into a situation that you're not really happy with, the one choice you can always make is: "Well, what am I going to do about this? How am I going to feel about this? Am I going to let this situation I find myself in here ruin the way I'm going to feel about myself for the rest of the day?" Absolutely not.

I once read something that I really liked on the back of an 18-wheeler truck. I was driving down Interstate 75 as I headed to Florida earlier this year to

Basketball Tryouts with Wally and The Undertaker

perform a week of shows. It read: "Life is what happens when you're busy making other plans." It is a famous John Lennon quote, and it's really true. Whatever choices you make will help create the situations you find yourself in. Here's a good example of how to or how not to create a situation through the choices you make. How many times have you been playing basketball maybe at a park, or a playground, or in gym class, and somebody comes over and tries to steal the ball from you? Instead of just trying to make a little poke at the ball or trying to jab the ball away from you, they make a huge karate chop crazy attack. In basketball, when somebody really goes out of their way to almost intentionally foul you by slapping you as hard as possible across the arms it's called the "Hack-a-Shaq." When someone does that, there's really no intention of getting the basketball. And if you play any basketball you'll know that this happens at least once a game: somebody on the other team really goes out of their way to get under your skin. Now as someone comes over and slaps you with two hands across the back of your arm while you're trying to shoot or pass the basketball, causing you to drop

> Q Mack

the rock, you've got a couple of choices you can make.

1) You can explode. You can lose your cool. You can absolutely freak out and maybe get aggressive by starting to make gestures or yell things at this person who gave you the old "Hack-a-Shaq."

2) The other choice, the more positive choice to make at this moment, is to shake it off and *keep your cool*. To realize in your head that it's better for the team, your coaches, and better for your personal safety to maintain your composure, take it back over to the bench, and remain focused. The foul has been called. You've got to let it go and keep your mind on the game.

There are so many times when you're playing street ball, where a player is so mentally off in his game. The reason they're so off or so mentally shaken is because of the choices that they've made. They've chosen to take the insult of the trash talking personally and let it affect their outlook and their attitude. *The biggest choice anybody has is the choice of attitude.* How am I going to react? How are *you* going to react to the situation that you find yourself in? That's *your* choice.

The Sleeping Bag 2

When I was in grade seven we went on a school trip up to the Muskoka Woods Resort, just outside of Muskoka, Ontario. There were about 14 or 15 grade seven boys staying in a log cabin with our teacher. Now, there was a guy in my class, Kyle, who decided that he was going to play a little joke on the kid in the class that nobody particularly liked. At that time, everybody kind of made fun of a couple of the kids in the class. Everybody got made fun of at times. That included a little bit of

> Q Mack

verbal bullying, a little bit of gang insult sessions that would go on at lunchtime. I was guilty of it as well. There are always one or two easier targets in every class and people tend to gang up on somebody who is a little more defenseless or a little different. Kids can go out their way, as I did at times, to make somebody feel bad. Put-downs, insults, clown sessions, jokes — it's all the same thing. And it's never a good thing.

We were up in Muskoka for a weekend trip, staying Friday and Saturday night and coming back on Sunday. On Saturday night, Kyle must have thought, "Well, I'm gonna show everybody else here in my class that I'm a joker, that I'm the number one prankster, that I'm fearless, that I'm creative. . . . I'm gonna increase my popularity in the classroom." That is what I think he was trying to do. I'm not sure what his incentive was, but his joke was to take this kid's sleeping bag — this poor kid that we all picked on — and to pee on it. He was going to straight up, soak this guy's sleeping bag by taking it outside and actually, well . . . you know . . . all over it. And I know a lot of us thought, "No, no that's too much. That's

The Sleeping Bag

going too far." But a couple of kids encouraged him, saying, "Yeah, do it. I dare you to. I double dare you to."

That's all it took for Kyle to take it outside and ... do it. So Kyle took the sleeping bag outside, came back in with the soaking wet sleeping bag, and threw it into the corner of the room.

Well, 10:30 at night came. We were all getting ready to shut it down for lights out at 11:00 p.m., and while everybody's getting their sleeping bag together, this poor kid grabs his sleeping bag, opens it up, and realizes very quickly that it smelled like my cat's litter box. It was just ridiculous. No one should have had to sleep in that, let alone touch it. And of course this kid didn't do anything to deserve it, he was simply an easy target. Everybody thought, "Ah, don't worry, he can take a joke. He's a tough kid." But really, it was an easy joke for everybody to score with.

So, of course a few dudes were laughing. A few other dudes felt bad, and this guy was really upset. He was a little bit mad, a little bit sad but mostly embarrassed and in shock that this actually happened to him. Embarrassed that some of the other kids were actually laughing.

Now, right away, somebody slipped the news to our teacher. Mr. Davies was a fair man and was always willing to give us the benefit of the doubt. As we'd seen in many situations, he would always ask a lot of questions to make sure he had the correct culprit. He came into the room and saw that this poor kid had a soaking wet sleeping bag.

"All right," Mr. Davies said. "I need to see everybody right here right now. I want everybody to stand here in front of me in a line-up."

So we all huddled in and he looked everybody in the eye and said, "Would the person who is responsible for this outrageous assault please step forward."

Now, everybody knew it was Kyle. But Kyle stood there with his eyes locked on the ground and didn't say a thing. Not one word. What Kyle should have done was put his hand up to say, "It was me," or to say "I'm sorry," or to somehow try to correct this mess that everyone was now a part of. It was silent for about two minutes before Mr. Davies said, "Well, I'm going to keep everybody here for 15 minutes. You

The Sleeping Bag

have 15 minutes to come into my room and confess that you were the one. I hope somebody here is man enough to confess that he is the one to blame for this crime and be man enough to take the punishment for it."

When Mr. Davies started off with the old "man enough to . . ." line, I thought, "Well Kyle's *definitely* going to have to fess up to this one."

Ten minutes passed and nothing happened. Finally, Mr. Davies came back in the room.

"Well, fellas, looks like somebody amongst you has chosen all of your fates. Because of one person's silence, all of your fates have been sealed. Tomorrow we will be getting up an extra hour and half early and going for a little jog around the beautiful Muskoka woods for some scenic views if you will. See you at 5:30 in the a.m."

Seems like some of my craziest adventures have taken place before 7:00 a.m.!

Mr. Davies left the room, and we all just sat there. Some people murmured, "Thanks a lot, Kyle," or "Thanks for nothing, Kyle," but Kyle went to sleep as though nothing was wrong. But something *was* wrong. Kyle had sold himself out. He had shown his true colours and everybody else realized it after that moment. In fact everybody realized it very clearly just a couple hours after that situation — because at five o'clock in the morning, in came Mr. Davies with a flashlight, flicking the lights on:

"UP AND AT 'EM, UP AND AT 'EM," he shouted, "LET'S GO LET'S GO. Here we go, grade seven, time to MOVE OUT. MOVE OUT. Time to SHIP OUT. Here we go. Everyone outside!"

Mr. Davies was definitely making sure that everybody here was going to receive an equal punishment until someone would step forward. Some justice had to be served. He couldn't tell this poor kid with the urine-soaked sleeping bag: "Sorry buddy, uh . . . couldn't find anybody to step up, but we're still looking into it." It's not a real encouraging thing to hear after your stuff gets messed with on a school trip.

As we all geared up to run around the beautiful Muskoka woods at 5:15 a.m., we all knew right then and there that Kyle could never be trusted. The other 14 dudes in that room, some of whom were supposed to be his friends, knew Kyle would sell everybody out

The Sleeping Bag

to save himself. In fact, he didn't really get to save himself because he had to run as well.

That following grade eight year was a lonely one for Kyle. That day Kyle sealed his own fate with his silence. He really picked up the tab and paid the price on the back end because that next year he was on the outside of all of the friendship circles. Suddenly, he was an outcast. Yet, it was by choice. The situation he found himself in was created by one negative or poor choice that he made — messing with this dude's sleeping bag. By trying to be the prankster, he ended up actually separating himself and earning distrust from everybody else in his class. That word went all the way to the girls, and both the girls and the guys in grade eight didn't have much time for this "prankster." Everyone knew at the drop of a hat he would save himself and lie.

The important thing I learned from that experience was that a lie can be executed with words or with *silence*. You don't have to say a word to blatantly lie to somebody, and the "silent lie" can be just as costly, just as hurtful, just as bad as the spoken lie. It's also important to keep in mind that a lie, whether

Q Mack

with words or with silence, can put you into serious situations. By choosing the lie — we're coming back to choices — you create the negative situation that you're in. *Telling the truth or telling a lie is about making a choice.* And in the case of a lie, it's not just one person who suffers. Think carefully. While choosing the lie might seem like the easy choice, it will come back to you and sometimes end up being far worse than any punishment that might come with telling the truth.

Saturday Morning Madness

The hardest working person I have ever met is my mother. She is an absolute phenomenon when it comes to work. My mom has worked for everything she has ever got in her life and continues to grind out what most people would consider an unbelievable schedule. I can't remember a time where my mom has worked less than 60 hours a week. Literally. I also can't remember a time where my mom has not put her best effort forward on any project she's ever undertaken or put her name to. My mom

> Q Mack

teaches grade five this year. She spent a couple years as a school principal, and about 25 years as a teacher. In the summertime, she is a university professor. And that's during her "summer break" when she's supposed to be relaxing. Instead, she goes up to Nipissing University for seven or eight weeks as a professor and teaches 150 or 200 aspiring teachers. She's also recently taken on a tutoring service. She bought a franchise about five or six years ago now and her job is to hire teachers and match them up with kids who need extra tutoring in certain subjects. She's gone out of her way to get almost 100 teachers working for her three or four shifts a week. So, she manages the "Little Extra Help Tutoring Service" on top of everything else. Now if that's not enough, she finds all the time in the world to be a "mother." She's been there for every basketball game we've ever played. She's hard to miss in the front row with her trumpet, a tambourine, an air horn, and wearing a T-shirt with our names on it. She schedules around our lives, all the while working 80 plus hours a week.

When my mom would tell my brother and me, "I want you to cut the lawn" or "I'd like you to help

Saturday Morning Madness

your dad clean the garage today," as much as we never wanted to clean the garage or shovel the driveway or cut the lawn, we'd do it. It's very tough to let somebody down who's working literally four times as hard as you are.

Saturday mornings at my house were work-a-thons. I don't know if this sounds familiar to anybody reading this right now, but on Saturday mornings, my mom had this little ritual. It went something like this:

The clock would strike 7:30 a.m. My mom would enter my brother's and my room and give us a little shake on the bunk beds and say "All right fellas! We need you out in the kitchen. I've got a list of things that need to be done this morning."

My brother and I were in shock. This *was* Saturday morning and it was a regular event, but every time it happened over nine or ten years, we were stunned that it was actually happening. If we didn't move, then we had the water gun to contend with. If we hadn't made it out of bed by a certain time, we could hear her filling up the Super Soaker in the bathroom, ready to give us a blast of cold water.

So, my mom woke us up at the unheard-of hour

> Q Mack

of 7:30 a.m. on a *weekend*, to do housework and yardwork. And there was always a list that would take us at least four hours to complete. My mom would have some breakfast waiting for us at 7:30. By 8 o'clock, the garden gloves were on. The toilet scrubbers were ready to go. The vacuum was charged up. The lawn mower was gassed up and ready to rock 'n' roll. I'm telling you right now, the jobs that my mom created for Saturday morning were way out of hand. If the lawn needed to be re-sodded, we were the guys. If the garage needed to be painted, we were the crew. If the pool needed to be drained and scrubbed down from the inside out with toothbrushes so the algae wouldn't build up for the next year, we were the pool men of the hour. We were the guys who did every job my mom could think of. My mom would say, "When you're done these jobs, you can go." But they were so well planned, and so well timed that you had to work at an 80 to 90 percent pace just to finish before noon. So, when all the good shows came on — the NBA *Inside Stuff* would come on right at the crack of noon — you were good to go.

When my friends finally got up out of bed at 11:30

Saturday Morning Madness

and called me to say, "So what do you want to do today? I'm *bored!* We should go to the *mall.* We should find something to do. There's *nothing* to do. I just woke up. I'm going to go back to bed 'cause I'm so tired," I would just think, "Are you *kidding me?* What, are you *serious* man? We've been up for five hours doing manual labour with *my mother!* I think I need to go to the mall right now, just to get a little stretch from all that gardening!" My friends always knew that Friday night was not a good night to sleep over at my house, because anybody who woke up at my house on Saturday morning — cousin, friend, neighbour sleeping over for a slumber party — was in on the housework session until it was done.

My mom is truly my hero because of her work ethic. I remember her going back to school to take a couple courses 10 or 15 years ago. I thought, "My mom's already a teacher. Why would she be taking these courses?" But every course she took would get her a little pay raise. She would be studying for some of these courses late into the night and at the same time baking six or eight apple pies for the school Christmas sale in order that I'd walk in having some

Q Mack

freshly baked pies. Some nights, my mom would be up until 3:30 in the morning only to arrive at her school later that morning, ready to function. By 8:15 a.m. she was there, smiling, ready to go. She's kept up this pace for over 25 years and there's nobody I know that works as hard as she does.

My mom is not a good person to pick strawberries beside or garden with or wash dishes in front of. She used to play this game with my brother, Tommy, and me when we were kids in order to get us "dudes" to do the dishes. She would say things like, "Well, I'm going to start washing these dishes here, and you two get a dish towel each and start drying. And if you can catch up to me you can stop and I'll dry the rest of them myself." We thought this was a sweet deal. My mom would wash two cups. We'd be starting to wipe down those two cups thinking we're gonna get out of here real quick, then she would slip a plate in the sink.

And we thought, "All right, all right. Just a plate. Just a plate. No problem."

So I'd grab the plate. The next thing you know there'd be two plates in there, then three plates. Then two more cups. And we'd just be catching up, think-

Saturday Morning Madness

ing "Oh yeah we got it. I've got a plate. Tommy's got a plate . . . sweet! We're right there. I think we're gonna catch up."

I would put my plate in the cupboard. Tommy's reaching up to put his plate back into the cupboard, and then my mom would get us . . . the silverware. Just as Tommy would reach over to put that last plate in the cupboard and just as we thought we'd won, she'd pull the old silverware card and toss about seven or eight forks — *BOOM* — smack dab into the middle of the dish rack. And we were pooched. Then plates followed, along with more cups and maybe some pots and pans, but at the end, we thought . . . "Wait a minute, my mom just created a little game for us to work hard."

She only has one mode, one speed — and that's overdrive. She's always moving ahead and being progressive. Her work ethic is twice and three times what most people would expect.

After I got to age 16, my mom started loosening the reins a little bit letting me sleep in 'til 11 o'clock on Saturday mornings like a normal kid. Those mornings were some of the best times of my life. I'd have a

> Q Mack

long day Friday after an early basketball practice, and a great sleep on Friday night. When I would turn and look at the clock on Saturday morning and it would say "8:30" and I was still in bed, I thought, "This is heaven! This is great! This is what I've been waiting for my whole life. My mom is finally turning into my friend and not so much just my mom anymore."

I think my mom is cool because she allows us to express ourselves, all the four kids in our family. While she works so hard, she only expects us to put forward a consistent, constant effort rather than work at her pace. My mom would never ever allow us to get in the habit of procrastinating. It was a tough lesson to grasp, but a valuable one. *Hard work and effort is necessary to succeed.* There's no other way to get ahead. Whether your goal is to become a top basketball trickster or make a school basketball team, it will only be achieved if you work hard at it. *If you want to succeed at something, you cannot be afraid of hard work.* It's amazing what you can achieve if you put effort into something. My mom, for instance. Not only is she the president of her own company,

Saturday Morning Madness

but she's a full-time grade school teacher, part-time university professor, and full-time mom. She's an incredible woman and a great example of how the value of hard work cannot be overlooked.

It Could Be Worse

My dad worked at Chicago Rawhide in Brantford for about 23 years. Chicago Rawhide is a factory which produces rubber and rubber products, and for years my dad worked there as an arbitrator. He was the "go-between" between the company and the workers' union. His job was to listen to what the workers thought about an issue, and then go talk to the company executives, bosses, and foremen to see what their opinion was on the same subject. Afterwards, my dad would go back to

Q Mack

the workers and tell them, "This is what they (the company exec's) think and this is why." He was responsible for keeping things cool, for keeping the lines of communication open between two parties. Therefore, he needed to convey points objectively without showing favouritism to either side. After delivering the arguments to both sides, he would then come up with quality, positive solutions . . . and really quite quickly, I might add. He would always remind me that every situation has to be looked at in its proper perspective.

I've always thought my household is a little different than other households, although I have heard of a number of families that operate similar to mine. My mom is the engine, the workhorse that really pushes the family. My dad is the super-glue that binds everyone tightly together, making sure all the loose ends are tied up. He pays attention to detail and has always, *always* helped us when it comes to dealing with stressful situations.

When I was entering a grade five speech contest, he was the first person to tell me how to get over the stage fright.

It Could Be Worse

"Even if there are fifty people in the crowd, that's okay. Just act like you're talking to one person. Talk to a group of people as you would talk to a person one-on-one. Picture her standing right in front of you," he said.

That stuck in my mind and it still does to this day. Now, when I get up to perform, instead of 50 people, I'm in front of 500, or even *5000* people at a time. And when I stand in front of those 5000 people, I still hear my dad's words. It can be really stressful to stand up in front of your whole school to give a speech or perform in a Christmas pageant or perhaps do something that maybe is a little out of your comfort zone.

Imagine you really wanted to make it on a basketball team, and now you're a starter. At the end of the game the coach tells you to take the final shot. And you think, "Aw, man, aw man. . . ." That's a bigtime pressure situation. Well, my dad is the one to sit down with you and say, "Let's think about this situation. Do you want to shoot the final shot?"

And you might think, "Well yeah, of course. I'd love it if the ball went in and I was the one to shoot it because everyone would think I'm a hero."

Then my dad would say, "Okay, but let's say that you miss? In fact, let's bank on the fact that you *are* going to miss. Are you still willing to take that shot if I'm telling you right now that you're going to shoot and miss it? Are you going to shoot now?"

Then you might say, "Well, no. I can't see where you're going with this. Of course I wouldn't shoot it. If I knew it wasn't going to go in, why would I shoot it?"

And my dad would tell you, "If you're afraid to shoot it, you're going to miss it anyway. If you're afraid to be in that position, if you're afraid to deal with that pressure or deal with that stress and you can't deal with the pressure properly, then it is going to beat you up and you are going to miss that shot. Try to bolster your confidence, try to bolster your ego a little bit and give yourself a little more credit."

When my dad and I had this conversation, I thought to myself, "Give yourself a little more credit. Hmmm."

He was quick to add, "You can give yourself *more* credit when you start *practising*."

My dad wasn't suggesting that I should go and

It Could Be Worse

inflate my ego. Rather, he suggested that I have more confidence in myself, that I give myself more credit after putting in more practice time. When you become more fluid or comfortable with certain skills, you become more comfortable with yourself when it comes to performing those skills. That's really what it comes down to. It's one thing to casually shoot the occasional free-throw in your driveway. It's only 15 feet away. Sure, I can make the ball go in the basket. Mission accomplished. It's a whole different animal when you're shooting that free-throw in front of 2000 screaming fans at the end of a city final game.

You may think to yourself, "Hey, this isn't the same as when I stood in my driveway."

Dealing with pressure, as my dad always said, is all about perspective. In this case, you may find these situations stressful because you haven't had enough practice. And the more out of practice you are, the more pressure you're going to feel. But if you spend a lot of quality time really focussing on your foul shots, then it will be a different story when you stand there in front of those fans. Think of it in perspective: the more you practise, the more comfortable you'll be in

> Q Mack

that situation. Then, when the coach wants you to take that final shot, you won't be afraid to say, "Yeah, sure I'll do it."

When we were outside practising free-throws in the driveway, Dad would always encourage us:

"Hey, the practice is going to pay off. Larry Bird was always a great free-throw shooter."

For Larry Bird, free-throw shooting was key. A lot of times the end of a game comes down to free-throw shots. Take a look at the free-throw stats at the end of the game. A team may have lost by three points. That same team missed *15 free-throws* that night. They could have won if they'd got those shots. But no . . . not enough people practise a small but vital part of the game. The small details help make up the big picture.

One tough situation I had was getting cut from a team. I was sitting at home, sulking and complaining. I went on about how the coach ripped me off, how it was all political, and I didn't make the team because the coach's wife hates me for being a prankster and this and that and this . . . everything I could think of. My dad just said, "Hey, could be worse."

> It Could Be Worse

And I thought, "What do you mean?"

"Hey, you should be thankful for what you have right now instead of complaining about what you don't have," he told me. "So you don't have a team to play on this summer. Big deal. You have a healthy body so you can improve with practice. Some people don't have the use of their arms or legs. You do. Work on your skills instead of complaining about why it didn't work out for you."

He was right. And I learned a lot that day about what is actually important.

I never hear my dad complain. He deals with things in their proper perspective. He understands that there is no point in letting situations control how he feels about things. Here is one favourite saying that my dad told me:

"Don't sweat the small stuff. And most of the time, it's ALL small stuff."

I know he did not make that saying up, but he is a shining, brilliant example of somebody who keeps things in perspective and "doesn't sweat the small stuff." There are certain things that you can't control, so why worry about them? You can't control what

> Q Mack

other people think about you so don't let that bring you down. There are many factors in life you can't change. You can't change anything about the weather, so why would you be upset when it's raining? To let a factor that you cannot control actually take control of your emotional state is as ridiculous as letting someone upset you for the hairstyle you've chosen. If I got upset every single time somebody looked at me and whispered to their friend and snickered about my hair, or my sunglasses or my wristbands or the colour of my shorts . . . my goatee, or the fact that I shave my legs . . . whatever it may be . . . if I get upset by their judgements then they win. If I changed myself to fit their expectation, I'd be making changes every day of my life! For every kid who said "that's so cool" to something I did, there'd be a kid who would say "who do you think you are?" I say . . . "Don't hate. Participate." To participate in being unique doesn't cost anything. And hey, it's a new way of looking at things!

What you *can* control, however, is your attitude. It all comes back to choices. Choose to keep things in perspective and choose to keep up a good attitude.

It Could Be Worse

My dad is comfortable with himself. He doesn't go out of his way to impress anyone. And because he's so comfortable with himself, everybody else feels comfortable with him. He's never one to judge. He doesn't make mountains out of molehills. Instead, he deals with things the way they should be dealt with. He looks at a situation from all angles, assesses the facts, and then makes a decision.

I can remember a time in high school when I was in grade 9 or 10, when I sat my dad down at the kitchen table.

"Dad, today at practice I lost my cool and punched my coach in the face 'cause I didn't like the play he was trying to set up for our team. I totally lost it and freaked out. So, I punched my coach in the face and I think I'm going to be kicked off the team. I also got suspended from school for a week."

My dad sat there with a shocked and angry look on his face.

"You WHAT?"

"I punched my coach in the face, I got suspended from school, kicked off the team, and I just thought you should know."

> Q Mack

My dad was in shock. He was about to lay down a serious punishment that would have probably sounded to the tune of me being grounded for about a month. Just as he was about to lay down the law, I said:

"Oh, Dad, by the way, I didn't really punch my coach in the face, I didn't get kicked off the team, and I didn't get suspended from school for a week. I did, however, get 54% on my math exam this semester and I just thought you should know that things could be a lot worse. I just wanted you to take this math situation in the proper perspective."

My dad smiled for about 15 seconds, and then said, "54% in math? We're going to have a little talk about this."

Needless to say, I had to get my average up to about 79 before the end of the school year if I wanted to see any kind of March break.

Sometimes, in the heat of the moment, it's really hard to put things in perspective. Before freaking out about something, try to look at it from a different angle. Okay, so it hurts to be cut from a team, but with practice, you can improve. Hey, at least you're lucky to

It Could Be Worse

even try out for the team! Yeah, it's scary to get up in front of a whole crowd of people, but you know what? They would probably feel exactly the same way as you do if they were in your shoes. So, instead of panicking, imagine yourself having a one-on-one conversation. Look for solutions to the problem rather than getting stuck and getting upset about it. Got a bad grade in math? Okay, so instead of being all upset about it, look at ways to fix the problem. Then, when you get that mark up, you'll feel a heck of a lot better. And no matter what, remember: *"It could be worse."*

Michael Jordan's Losing Streak

When I was in grade six, and my younger brother, Tommy, was in grade four, we would go over to Wood Street Park in Brantford which is close by our house. We'd go over and shoot jumpers for hours. On many occasions, there was another set of brothers or friends who wanted to play us two-on-two. There was one set in particular who were about three years older than us. So we'd play these guys and lose about 11 to 1. We played these guys on and off for

Q Mack

a couple of weeks and lost consistently. And we could never find a way to beat these guys. I eventually thought we should stop trying and just play other people. But any time these guys wanted to play, we'd play them. And we'd always lose.

Now we played these dudes on and off for the next three years and as we got older so did they. By the time we were in grade eight/nine they were in grade ten/eleven and were still beating us pretty easily. But instead of quitting, instead of giving up and deciding that we could never beat these guys, my brother and I kept practising and kept playing. When I was in grade nine, we could finally start competing and actually winning games against these guys who were now in grade twelve/thirteen. It was such a big accomplishment for my brother and me to actually start beating these guys who we had lost to for so many years.

I can relate to how Michael Jordan felt in the late '80s. He had been in the NBA for seven years at this point and his Chicago Bulls had lost consistently to the Detroit Pistons . . . in 1987 then '88 and '89. In 1990 his team lost again to the Pistons in the confer-

Michael Jordan's Losing Streak

ence finals. It was painful to watch. *Finally*, in 1991, Michael Jordan and the Chicago Bulls (my favourite team and favourite player at the time) went all the way to the championship. As Michael Jordan hugged the final game MVP basketball trophy, he cried. I think a lot of the emotion came from remembering how many times he had failed and how many times that he had to bounce back. It paid off.

There was a Nike commercial with Michael Jordan where he talked of how many times he had failed.

"I have failed hundreds of times in my career. I have missed many shots and lots of game winners and I've let my team down several times because I've not come through. I've failed over and over and over in my career. And that is why I succeeded."

What I learned from that Michael Jordan quote was that it was learning from all the failures that created the success. It was the combination of growing from the mistakes, trying to keep things in perspective, bouncing back from failures, being resilient, persevering, and keeping up the determination . . . that was what led to the success. Whenever the going

Q Mack

gets tough, the trick is to be able to bounce back and try your hardest. Try not to quit, not to get frustrated, not to get stressed out. Instead, keep things in perspective. Get up and try again. Failure is going to happen. We're all going to mess up. That's cool. We've got to get used to that. *It's all right to mess up, it's just not all right to give up.* Hey, Michael Jordan did it. So can you.

Bouncing back from failure is maybe the most important point because we deal with overcoming obstacles or the fear of failure on a daily basis. Making the choice to continue working at something or to quit altogether is pretty much something we face day in and day out. I believe the only time a person truly fails is when s/he stops trying or quits. There's no back end on how many times you try to achieve something. You can succeed at anything you want so long as you know that it's okay to fail. Don't let that stop you from trying.

Now, I think that you should know that *everyone will fail in his or her lifetime,* so get used to it. Everyone comes up short on a daily basis in one area or another. I don't know if it's possible to go 24 hours

Michael Jordan's Losing Streak

without slipping up on something. There is always something you could have done a little bit better or put a little more effort into. I think everybody just has to get used to the fact that failure is a part of life. More importantly, it's okay to fail. It's okay to mess up. It's okay not to be good at something as long as you *don't stop trying*. How you deal with the setbacks will distinguish you and being able to bounce back from failure is a huge asset. It's a giant step towards being comfortable with yourself. It's okay to look a little bit foolish sometimes. It's all right to look silly.

I don't mind getting myself into situations that are maybe a bit more stressful for other people. For example, I remember a newspaper reporter asked me one time, "Q, I cannot believe that you stand in front of 1,000 people and talk while shooting a half-court shot. What do you do if you miss it in front of everybody?"

"What do I do if I miss it? I shoot it again."

He looked at me for a second, then said, "You shoot it again?"

"You have to understand," I told him. "I really do not have any fear of messing up. I'm quite comfortable with it. I'm not concerned with it because I realize that I will mess up on occasion. I do miss shots. *Things don't always work out well, and that's okay. When you fail, try again.* But when you throw in the towel and say, 'I'm done,' that's really the only time that you fail."

Johnny, the Ladies, and the Trip to McDonald's

A few years back, I was in Orlando, Florida, for spring break. I was about 18 or 19 years old. My friends and I were at a classic spring break party where everybody was pretty rowdy and the party went on late into the night. Now my friends and I had decided that we would go to the party, hang out and have a good time, but we made a pact between us that no matter what kind of peer pressure was going down, alcohol wasn't the way to go. Our thought was that we didn't need booze to have a good time.

Q Mack

Now, we're at this party, we're hanging out, everything's cool. Johnny, one of the dudes who I had met that week, was a college student. He drove down to Orlando in his SUV for the week. Well, it was getting a little late and he had been consuming a fair amount of alcohol all night. The next thing you know, he's saying, "I'm driving over to McDonald's! Who's gonna come with me? Yeah! It's not that far, it's only across the road. Who wants a piece of the action?"

Well, I looked at some of my friends and thought, "Nope. Not me. There's no way I'm getting in the car with this dude. He's been drinking, he wants to jump behind the wheel, and he's in the mode to show off."

I knew he was in the mode to show off because there were some young ladies who showed up at the party. These pretty girls had started to flirt a little bit with some of us, including this drunken idiot who's yelling about McDonald's to everyone.

Now a few of these girls answered: "Yeah, we'll go to McDonald's."

I walked over to them and said, "Ladies, I don't want to burst your bubble, but this guy here, Johnny, has been drinking for the last couple of hours. I don't

> Johnny, the Ladies, and the Trip to McDonald's

know if you want to be going anywhere with him."

The girls went over to Johnny. "Johnny, are you all right?" they asked. "Are you good to drive? Are you okay?"

And Johnny said, "Yeahhhh, man! I'm cool. I'm good to go, man. I'm good to drive."

The ladies turned to me. "Johnny seems to be all right. Let's go! Q, you coming?"

I'm looking at these girls and I'm thinking, "Man, this decision is tougher now than it was before when it was just Johnny who wanted to go to McDonald's. Now the girls are involved. If I don't go, are these girls going to think I'm not cool? Are they going to think that I'm scared?" But then I thought, "I don't know if this is a situation I want to get myself involved with."

So, I turned around and ask my friends for their opinion on the whole scenario, but two of my friends had taken off to the beach. Another friend was deep in conversation with a young lady. Suddenly, I realized I'm alone with Johnny and these three girls.

"C'mon, man," Johnny said, "we'll all go to McDonald's! It's gonna be crazy, man! We got new

Q Mack

CD's. We're gonna party on the way to McDonald's, and hook it up big time."

I'm still thinking, "I don't know," even though the three girls were encouraging me.

"C'mon, Q. C'mon. It's just going to be three minutes. We're gonna be right back, we're gonna be real quick. It's not going to be a problem."

At that point I finally thought, "You know what? When it comes down to it, I really don't care what these girls think of me and I could care less what Johnny thinks of me. If these guys don't think I'm cool for saying no, then that is their problem."

For one, I knew getting into a car with Johnny was not safe. Getting into a vehicle with anyone who has consumed alcohol is crazy. Stupid stupid stupid decision.

So I told Johnny, "Sorry brother, I'm out."

"Can I pick you up something on the way?" he asked.

The girls agreed, "Yeah, we'll grab something for you."

"Naw, forget it," I said.

I didn't want to be involved in this situation, but I

Johnny, the Ladies, and the Trip to McDonald's

also didn't want to support them going by giving them some money to come back with a couple of hamburgers or a sundae. By getting them to pick something up for me, I would be encouraging them to go to McDonald's with an intoxicated driver. I would now be involved in putting them in a bad position.

I said, "Ladies, maybe I'll catch up with you later on. Johnny I'll talk to you tomorrow, I hope."

Before they left, I gave him the quick, "Are you sure you're good to drive, man? I don't think you should be driving anywhere right now. Why don't you just stay here and party? Why don't you just hang out for a bit."

Suddenly I realized what a good opportunity I was in. I had the chance to try and turn this situation around instead of just walking away from it. I was showing my individuality by saying "no" to that kind of peer pressure. At the same time, I realized maybe that's just not enough. Maybe it's just not sufficient to say, "You guys have a good time, I'm out of here," and completely withdraw from the situation. Instead, I thought maybe I could help correct the situation as I saw it.

> Q Mack

So I started to talk to Johnny a little bit, stalling him from leaving. We talked about his vehicle first, then the conversation turned to basketball. Five minutes later we were sitting at the table debating whether or not Michael Jordan is the best player of all time. Then, I told him about Brantford, and how Wayne Gretzky is the Michael Jordan of my city. We talked back and forth for the next 15 minutes until the girls got a bit restless and split. Johnny and I just sat there. We talked for another 25 minutes about all kinds of things. At the same time, I asked another dude at the party to call and order us a bunch of take-out food.

This was a great opportunity to not only step out of a situation and show some individuality, but to step right back into it with positive intentions of turning it around. The worst possible scenario would have had Johnny jumping into his vehicle and taking off with the girls. They may have got in trouble with the law or worse, got into a car accident. My thought was not to start a fight, or argue with him. Instead, I kept talking to him, distracting him from taking off to his car.

I was lucky. It worked out really well. It was a

People are entitled to their own opinion and when it comes to the way I look, there are many, many opinions. Now, I go out of my way every day to be intentionally different from anyone else. If you see me on any given day of the week, you're going to find me looking a little bit different from everyone else, whether it be my hair or the way I'm dressed. But that's not what sets me apart from everybody else. My flashy, crazy, unique "look" is only a piece of the puzzle. *Being an individual, as far as I'm concerned, is about making your own decisions.* Now I'm not talking about setting your own rules or behaving however you want whenever you want. Being an individual does not entitle you to act out of line. That's not what it's all about. *What it is about is making smart decisions for yourself rather than just following along with what everyone else is doing.*

good situation to show some individuality. Sometimes they're not as easy as that. In high school, there are many situations where you may be at party where there are substances floating around and somebody intoxicated decides to jump into his or her car either alone, or with friends. It's a dangerous, dangerous situation to get yourself into. The thing to remember is that it is an *avoidable* situation.

A big part of individuality is showing that you're not afraid to be different. It's not just about throwing elastics in your hair, or having a crazy beard, or wearing funky clothes. It's what you do in your daily life. What kind of actions you are willing to take. You really have to look at yourself in the mirror and think, "Do I really care what everyone else thinks of me? How do I feel about myself?" I've often found that it's the people who are always concerned with other people's opinions that get into these dangerous situations. Sometimes the issues are small: "Should I show up wearing this hat? Or will people think it's not cool?"

Sometimes, they may be more significant: "Everyone is drinking. If I don't, does that mean I won't be accepted?"

And sometimes, deadly: "Okay, so he's had a few drinks, but I'm sure he's okay to drive and everyone else is going, so..."

It comes down to that root problem of letting the actions or opinions of other people influence your decision. Influence is a huge part of individuality. If you let yourself be influenced badly, the consequences can be very serious. Part of being an individual is looking at all aspects of a situation in order to make a responsible decision . . . even if it's not a popular one.

Okay, let's get serious here. Let's talk about individuality. Individuality, to me, is the art of being unique. It is the opportunity to be a little bit different, a little bit creative. It's what sets you apart from everyone else. Yes, individuality can include the way you walk, talk, act, or dress, but true individuality starts from within. It is about how you feel about yourself and how high your confidence level is. It is about having distinct character and being independent.

Being an "individual" is really, in my opinion, the most fun anyone can ever have. It provides me with daily entertainment. When I walk into a mall with my 35 bleached-blond braids sticking up into a[ir] and my matching bleach-blond goatee nicely bra[ided], I get some serious looks, and that's only the be[gin]ning. My sideburns are shaped just "so." Even the [rest] of my beard is shaved into a specific pattern. [I'm] wearing colour-coordinated gear, with match[ing] headwear — whether it be a headband, bandanna, [or] visor — and the absolute essential ingredient: su[n]glasses. I like to have my fat Nike watch on my le[ft] wrist, and maybe wear chains around my neck. M[y] look, from the average person's perspective, i[s] absolutely absurd. I get stares, comments, and double-takes. I turn heads everywhere I go. And this happens every single day. At the library, gas station, mall, video store, grocery store . . . it doesn't matter. Everyone seems to have an opinion about my look. Of course, because I'm usually wearing sunglasses, no one can really see where my eyes are looking. So, they don't realize that I can see their reaction. Everyone has a comment to make. Sometimes I get a smile, sometimes a chuckle. Sometimes it's a wife turning to her husband to say, "My Goodness, I hope our son never turns out like that!"

Major Influencer??

In grade eight, I had risen to a point in my school where I was in a real position of influence. Everybody in the school knew that I was a basketball player at this point. I had been practising, so my shot was getting a bit better and my tricks were coming along well. I was perceived as being "cool" by the kids in school. I took this newfound power — influence — as an excuse to do whatever I want. I thought, "Aw man, everybody's going to do what I tell them to do? Everybody thinks what I think is cool? Well, sweet. Hey! I can start harassing or picking on whomever I want to. I'll start calling shots around here, and do my thing. Throw my weight around. These kids will do whatever I say because I've got the ability to influence them!"

I thought having influence was going to be sweet. I was going to use this power to my advantage. But I wasn't truly influencing them; instead I was manipulating them. Manipulation is a negative form of influence. Negative influence is, of course, encouraging people to do the wrong things. And in grade eight, I had my moments where I was being a bad influence on others.

One time, in my English class, while we were working on pronouns, predicates, adverbs . . . elements of grammar, my teacher asked a question and I wasn't really listening. I was in the back talking with my buddies. And of course the teacher had to ask us a couple of times to be quiet. We kept quiet for about thirty seconds then went back to talking and a little bit of note passing. The teacher finally raised her voice and said:

Major Influencer??

"Quincy Mack, do you think you already know everything there is to know about the English language?"

My thought was, "Sweet. September is here. It's time for me to flex a little of my influence on this class right now and let them know who's running the show."

So I said, "Absolutely."

And she said, "Oh you do, do you? Maybe you'd like to take over and teach the class from here."

So I thought, "All right. Here we go."

Everybody else started to laugh and look directly at me and I thought now would be a great time to stand up and walk to the front of the class and show the room what I'm made of.

So I stepped up to the front of the classroom, and started spouting some ridiculous nonsense for 15 or 20 seconds. By the 30 second mark, my teacher had had enough. The kids were laughing. I was making no sense, just clowning around and showing off. So, my teacher sent me directly to the principal's office.

Now I was sitting out there for 10 minutes waiting

Q Mack

to speak to the principal. While I was sitting in my chair, I was thinking, "Ah, no worries. So what? I'm just gonna make an excuse. I'll make up some story as to why it went down like that. I'll try to blame somebody else or shift the story around so it doesn't make me look like the bad guy."

The principal opened his door. "All right, I'm ready to see you Quincy, come on in."

I sat down across from him. Our conversation was very short and very direct. The principal looked me in the eye and said this: "Quincy, you're one of the coolest guys in the school this year. You know that, right?"

I was taken aback by that. I didn't want him to think that he had said something that actually shook me a little bit, so I tried to shrug it off and said, "Yeah, well, I don't know. Whatever. Yes, some people might think I'm cool. Whatever."

"No no no," he said. "Everybody here thinks that you are one of the coolest kids in this school. Even the little kids. I was talking with the teachers a lot in the summer time and your name was one that came up quite often as a major influencer in our school this year."

Major Influencer??

I thought, major influencer? What are these teachers talking about behind my back? I wasn't even sure if they were calling me names or not. I'd never heard of someone being referred to as a "major influencer" before.

I said, "Oh, is that right?"

The principal went on to say, "Absolutely. Every kid in this school looks up to you. Everything that you do, these kids in grade four, five, and six want to start doing."

I was silent. The principal continued, "Every time you clown around, these little kids think, 'If Q's fooling around, I can do the exact same thing.'"

I thought, "Well I wasn't clowning around just to make other people clown around. I was just trying to get a few laughs. I was just trying to keep things loose. I was just trying to set a reputation for myself inside my class strictly with my own grade eight classmates. I was just trying to set a precedent early in the year by letting everybody know that I've got a rep to live up to."

My principal brought to my attention that everybody in the school was somehow watching me from a distance to see how I was going to act in certain situations. Now, I thought, "Okay, so what? Everybody's looking at me, wanting to know how I'm going to act . . . whatever. No big deal. So what? Now everybody's watching me be a clown. Now I have a bigger audience."

My principal then said something that absolutely floored me and made me go, "Uh, oh." And I didn't like it. I still don't like it when somebody tells me something that really catches me off guard.

My principal looked me in the eye and said, "Oh, by the way, Q? If you end up in my office one more time this year for a behavioural problem, or an attitude-related problem, then we're going to have a talk about your participation on the basketball team this year."

It was as though somebody hit me on the forehead with a frying pan. My nostrils cleared, my ears seemed wide open, as did my eyes.

I said, "Excuse me? The basketball team?"

And he said, "Oh, yes. If you're in this office anymore this year for an attitude-related problem or for trying to influence people negatively, we'll have to

Major Influencer??

talk. You've got to understand, Q, that the influence you have is more powerful than 90 percent of the things that the teachers or myself will try to enforce this year. Why? Because most of the kids in this school see the teachers, even me, as being the enemy or being somehow here specifically to enforce rules. And that's not really why were here. We're trying to let everybody grow and do their thing and express themselves, but we still have to play inside these rules. Now Q, you're one of the biggest influencers in this school. I don't want to have to kick you off the basketball team. You're the best basketball player in this school. This is not something I want to have to do, but we will do it if it came down to it."

Right then and there, I knew he was serious. I also knew that regardless of whether or not I was the best player in the school, he would have barred me from basketball or any athletic activities for that matter if I didn't start using this newly found power of influence in a positive way.

So I did. I absolutely did. I just started turning it around. Instead of teasing people in the playground and using influence to get people to gather around

Q Mack

and make fun of somebody, I started saying, "C'mon guys, let's go get into some hoop or this game of baseball, or whatever."

Doing something constructive inside the rules that was for everybody's good . . . this was what I focussed on. I desperately wanted to play basketball that year. I needed to play basketball. I couldn't be banned from the team, so what I was doing was for my own good as well. And I also found out that it actually helped other people. Other students were actually looking up to me. Little kids would actually start to believe that "If Q is doing it like this, there's no reason why I can't."

Being an individual means you're not afraid to be different. You're not afraid to do your own thing. Influence is a little bit different. Influence, to me, is your power to change people's minds. If you are capable of influencing people, not only can you change people's minds, but you can actually change their actions. When I sat at the party talking to Johnny, what I was doing was influencing him to stay in the house and out of his vehicle which would help to keep him safe. I was trying to influence him into making a responsible decision. He did.

Now "influence" is not the same as "manipulation." Manipulation is getting somebody to do something for your personal gain regardless of what the consequences for that person might be. As long as you profit from their action, you don't care if they get hurt. In Johnny's situation, if I'd played the "manipulation card" it might have looked like this:

"Johnny, while you're at McDonald's, grab us a few burgers. Actually, stop in at 7/11 for us and grab us a couple of Big Gulp slurpees as well."

That would have been manipulation because I'd be getting him to do a personal favour for me regardless of what consequences might have befallen him. Influence is bit different. Influence is the power, pull, or clout you have with other people. Not everyone has the same degree of influence. Still, those who have the power to influence others have an amazing gift.

Do you really want to be cool? Use your influence to help others and encourage people to take the positive

Q Mack

route. While it took my principal laying things on the line for me to change my attitude, I gained more from using my "influence" for good than I ever would have if I'd taken the negative route. You'd be surprised how powerful influence can be. Be smart. Use it wisely.

There's No Such Thing as a Perfect Player

Everybody would tell me when I was in grade two or three, "Set goals for yourself! Strive to achieve the best." One of our mottoes at school was "Strive to achieve excellence." But it was just a saying. It was just something I heard. It meant nothing to me until I wanted to become good at basketball. Right away I thought, "If I could become better at basketball, then maybe kids wouldn't laugh at me so much. If I could become better at basketball, maybe I could make the team and make some friends. If

> Q Mack

I could become better at basketball, maybe I could gain the respect of a couple of the older guys on the high school team."

Even when I was in grade six, I was always thinking about the high school players and how good they were at the game. At the gym, or the YMCA or the park or playground, I would wish that some of these older kids would say, "Hey, this little dude's all right. We should pick him for our team." I just wanted to be included. I thought, "Man, if I could actually get picked for one of the teams with the older guys that I thought were so cool at the time, that would be the best! If they would pick me to play with them, that would be sweet."

So, I began with an end in mind: to become a better basketball player. More specifically, a better shooter.

When I was in grade eight, I'd go out to my driveway with a pencil and a notepad. I realized that it was one thing to come out to the driveway and just shoot some random jump shots, do a few lay-ups, a few free-throws, sometimes some three-pointers, just aimlessly shoot the ball around. But when I went

There's No Such Thing as a Perfect Player

inside, I'd think, "I don't really know if I'm getting better at shooting or not. Sometimes it goes in, but not all the time. Most of the time it clanks off the rim." One of every seven or eight shots would actually find its way to the bottom of the basket.

I started to think, "How am I going to know if I'm getting better or not? How am I actually going to know if I'm doing better at shooting?" So I thought about it and clued in: "I want to become a better shooter, so I guess that's my goal. That's my big goal."

My major goal was to become a great shooter. If I could walk into a gym and just start firing it away from here, from there, from the corner, from half court to the other side of the gym . . . if I could just find a way to always put the ball in the bottom of the basket, man! That would be awesome! I'd love it. Everybody else would love it. So that was my goal.

But here's how it all started. I walked into the driveway every day, pen and paper in hand, thinking, "All right. If my major goal is to become a great shooter, that's a pretty big leap from where I am now. Right now, I'm not a very good shooter. So, I'm going to start standing right here. Right about at the foul

Q Mack

line about 15 feet away from the basket. I'm going to shoot a hundred shots here and figure how many shots are going in, and how many shots are missing the basket."

The first day I was out there, I scored a pathetic 12 out of 100. Now, at the time I shot with both my elbows flared out to the side and my feet would fly behind me a little bit when I jumped. It was a pure chest shot, not a textbook shot by any stretch of the imagination. So I considered my score of 12 out of 100 and thought, "That's brutal, buddy." But you have to start somewhere. At least I knew now how many balls were going in out of 100 shots. So, I wrote it down. Day one: 12 out of 100.

On day number two, I looked at my little notepad and I thought, "All right. Another 100 shots today." I know 100 shots sounds like it would be a lot to shoot, but really it only takes about 20 minutes. Even if you're rebounding by yourself, you can get 100 shots off in 20 minutes. Sometimes I'd convince my little brother Tommy to come out to the driveway and help rebound. Otherwise I was on my own, shooting with a goal in mind.

There's No Such Thing as a Perfect Player

Out on the court on day number two, I thought, "Okay, the first day, I got 12 out of 100. I can do better than that. I'm going to see if I can get at least 15 in today. It's better than 12." I shot the 100 jumpers or set shots and I ended up with a score of 16.

"Yeeeaaah," I thought. "Perfect. At least I reached my goal of 15."

So I wrote 16 down for day number two, even though my goal was only 15. I was excited. I got 16 and that was pretty sweet.

Day number three I decided that I should shoot for 20. And I shot my 100 shots. The problem was I didn't score 20; I scored 17. On day four I lucked out. I was still on 20, and wouldn't move until I made 20 baskets. Only problem was, I shot a pathetic 13. On day number five, I went out to the driveway and shot 18. Still not 20. This went on for another week and I still couldn't make 20 baskets.

I started to get a little bit frustrated and upset. I began to think, "Wait a minute. This whole goal setting thing is not all it was cracked up to be. I thought this was going to help me get better. I don't see me getting any better. I don't know if this is really work-

> Q Mack

ing out. Maybe I'm just going to quit. Maybe I'm just going to go back to my old routine of just shooting around randomly. At least then I won't know if I'm getting worse."

Fortunately for me, the next day I went out and actually scored 21! And was I excited. I finally reached my goal of 20. Now I kept up this process of goal setting through grades 8, 9, 10, and all the way through high school. Every year I continue this process.

By grade nine I was shooting for 30 to 35 baskets out of 100. By the end of grade nine I was up to 35/40. I was no longer shooting from the foul line at this point; I was starting to back up. One step at first, then two steps, then three. I backed out to about 19 foot 9 inches (that's the official measurement for a college line. It's just under seven meters). Soon I was shooting for 45 out of 100. At this point I thought, "This is sweet. Almost every other shot goes in." Not quite one out of two, but it was getting there.

By grade 11, I was shooting in about 50 to 55 percent, and it was great! I started thinking back to when I was scoring 12, 15 . . . even 20. And that was only about three or four years before! It was awe-

There's No Such Thing as a Perfect Player

some to know that I was two, three, four times as good of a shooter as I was in grade seven. I kept up this process. Every time I went out to my driveway or to a gym, a playground, a schoolyard . . . wherever I could find a hoop, I'd shoot 100 shots and keep track of how many went in and how many missed.

Now today, while standing 20 feet from the basket, I score about 80 to 85 out of 100. In an NBA game, if you look at any of the stats, you'd realize that the best three-point shooters in the game are only shooting about 40 to 45 percent. It's unheard of for somebody to be shooting over 50 percent in an NBA season. But that's also a game situation. You aren't wide open, all by yourself in a comfortable little gym with no pressure or paycheck on the line. This was just me and the basket. And in a casual situation I can score about 80/85 out of 100. It all started back with scoring 12 and 15.

The process of goal setting is a super important one. It's a key component of becoming better at anything. The process of goal-setting is this: *A bunch of little goals achieved = one major goal accomplished.*

Sure, a lot of people say, "I already know that.

Q Mack

Goal setting is good to do. Fine." It's one thing to hear it. It's a completely different animal to put the actual process into action. Once you practise goal setting it is absolutely incredible to observe the results and see how far you can get. The people who actually want to accomplish something great, these people start setting goals very very early. Is it about luck? I don't think so.

Look at somebody like Tiger Woods, or Michael Jordan. People think, "Man, those dudes are so lucky! They make all this money, they get to travel, they get to be on TV. . . ." They get to do this and that. But that's not just about luck. It wasn't until high school that I started to realize that luck had very little, if any, part of it. Predetermined goal setting with an end in mind is key. Tiger Woods began playing golf when he was four years old and he knew by the time he was seven or eight that he wanted to be a professional golfer. True, his dad had a lot to do with keeping him on track, but there's also a certain time where you decide for yourself, "Is this is what I really want to do? Do I really want to continue with this practice? Do I want to keep it up?" Whether it's basketball or

There's No Such Thing as a Perfect Player

piano lessons or working with animals . . . whatever it is that you find yourself interested in right now. There comes a time where you start making your own decision.

For me, it was the shooting. That's the first goal I set for myself. I still do it today. My goals today, though, aren't necessarily to become a better shooter. Right now, one goal of mine is to learn one new trick every month. Every month, one brand new trick. Whether it be a basketball trick, a sleight of hand magic trick, a balancing trick, a juggling trick, a trick shot . . . it doesn't matter. I want to learn one new trick every month. My thought is this:

"There are 12 months in a year. If I learn one every month then in five years I'll know 60 new tricks."

Now sometimes I like to learn two or three new tricks, but my bare minimum goal is one trick a month. At the end of the year I have 12 brand new, fresh tricks. It's just a small goal I've set for myself, but every day that ticks by in a month . . . I think, "Uh oh. I haven't started to work on my new trick yet and it's already October the 12th. Better get on it."

Q Mack

It's very important not to procrastinate. Goal setting should start today. As you're reading this book right now you should be thinking, "Time to set some goals! Right now is the best time!" Not next year or when you're in an older grade. Not in a couple of years when you're in high school, or university, or college. Come on, now, you know I'm right. You need to start setting goals for yourself, *now*.

Becoming Canada's best basketball trickster wasn't something I decided when I was 24. I didn't sit down two years ago and say, "Yeah, you know what? I'd be kind of cool to do some tricks and just slap it together and see how it works." No, I started thinking about this when I was 13.

"You know what'd be cool? It'd be cool if I could be on the Harlem Globetrotters. It'd be awesome to be on TV one time. Or to get a shoe contract the way Michael Jordan has a shoe contract. Any time Michael Jordan wants some shoes, he doesn't have to pay for them or worry about the colours. He just has to make a phone call and they send them to his house! Now, that would be sweet. That would be the coolest."

There's No Such Thing as a Perfect Player

And instead of just thinking, "Man, Jordan is lucky. That guy has it all." Instead of wishing, or hoping, I started dreaming and setting realistic goals I could achieve. Small goals at first, but once those get accomplished you're that much closer to achieving your major goal. You've got to start with some small achievable steps, something you can reach.

Another important thing with goal setting to keep in mind: don't worry about what everyone else is doing, or what everybody else thinks or has to say. Don't let that be your concern. What you should be concerned with is this: personal progress. *You* are getting better. Personal progress is key. It doesn't matter how good of a shooter your friend is, or how high this kid can jump or how fast another kid can run. That shouldn't be your concern. You've got to be concerned with *you*. Be concerned with your personal improvement, not the improvement of everyone else around you.

Adults do it all the time: "Oh, this guy has a sweet job," or "I wish I drove the car that she drives." Instead of wishing and comparing yourself to other people all the time, it's a lot more important to look in the mirror. Start improving yourself and setting goals for growth. Goal setting is the vehicle that will drive all of your dreams. You sit back and start dreaming about what you want to be, where you want to live, what you want to do, and why. Then, think about it. You may have set some pretty big goals, but the important thing to ask yourself is, "What can I do today? What smaller goals can I achieve today to reach that big goal?"

It's one thing to dream and to wish and to hope, but it's a whole new ball game when you start to put your dreams into action. In my opinion, over 80 percent of the world right now think it's impossible to pursue their dreams. I'm here to tell you right now that anything is possible with proper goal setting. It's an ongoing process, though. It never stops or ends. Once you reach a goal, do you walk out of the gym and say "I'm the best shooter in the world?" No. You raise that bar higher! Shoot for the stars! You know what? There's no such thing as a perfect shooter. The best shooter in the world is not a perfect shooter. He still misses shots. You're always going to have to try to

There's No Such Thing as a Perfect Player

get better. You might score 40 points one time or have six slam dunks ... but you didn't have a perfect game because you still missed a free-throw. You still turned the ball over.

There is such a thing as a flawless performance, but there's no such thing as a *perfect player.* You go out in baseball and pitch a perfect game. You can step up to a pool table and clear the whole table, or you can stand at a free-throw line and get 100 out of 100. That doesn't mean you're a perfect player. With that in mind, striving for perfection isn't really the goal. What we should strive to do with our goal setting is to become better and improve.

When people ask me about my basketball tricks, I just say, "Hey — I just want to become better than I was yesterday. I don't care if I become the best trickster that ever lived. I don't care if I'm the best trickster in the world. That's not my concern. My concern for me, personally, is to become better than I was yesterday. I'm not here to compare myself to this guy or that." Everybody wants to gauge themselves against the best in the world, and gauging to see where you stand is one thing, but my goal is never to be the "best who ever lived." If it happens, great, but that is not my personal goal.

There are some goals that aren't realistic. If you're a rapper or a singer and sell 30 million copies of your record, great. But how do you set that as a goal? That's out of your control. Now to set the goal that you're going to become a better singer/rapper than you were last week, that is accessible. As long as I'm constantly improving and setting my goals just a little bit higher every time, that's all I'm ever concerned with.

Goal setting is the only vehicle that I've ever known when it comes to getting better at something. Practising is great. When you practise something, you will definitely improve. The problem with simply practising without any structure or end result is that random amounts of practice with no set goal in mind are like spinning your wheels in the mud. You might be moving a little bit, but you're not getting anywhere with any type of speed or efficiency.

I found goal setting to be the ultimate way to achieve all of your dreams. Today my job involves

There's No Such Thing as a Perfect Player

working with teams like the Toronto Raptors, with Nike, with the NBA, and a lot of my friends always say the same thing to me:

"Q, you're so lucky, man. You're so lucky! You get all this gear for free, you travel all around the world, you get to meet all these cool famous people. You're so lucky!"

And I say, "Thanks man, that's kind of you to say. Thanks."

But in my head I keep thinking, "Lucky. Lucky? You call this lucky? You think I woke up one morning and all of a sudden said, 'Wow. It's the weirdest thing, Mom! I can spin a basketball on top of six broom handles as I balance it on my chin. It's the strangest turn of events and it only just happened to me.'"

Nope. Absolutely not. My mom has always been the one to tell me that you start with an end in mind. You don't just begin something randomly and say, hey let's give this a run for a bit. Let's see how this one pans out. *If you want results, you start with an end in mind then take it one step at a time.*

M.J. and The Great One

You wouldn't expect anybody to come out of Brantford, Ontario, Canada — Wayne Gretzky's hometown — to become a freestyle basketball player. Growing up eight blocks away from "The Great One" you soon see the effect that a hometown celebrity can have on an entire city. I don't know if there's a hockey player in the world who hasn't been influenced by Wayne Gretzky. But in Brantford specifically, all the kids and a large portion of adults, look up to the Gretzky family, and so they

> Q Mack

should. It's exciting really to have a celebrity or superstar from your hometown.

In grade five, everybody who I went to school with wanted to be a hockey player. All they would talk about was hockey. They'd trade hockey cards at lunchtime and go to hockey practice after school, even in the summer time. All year round, everybody would play hockey.

Except for me.

In grade three I discovered that I didn't really like skating as much as everybody else did. I think it was because I never learned how to skate backwards. If I had learned how to skate backwards at a younger age, who knows? Maybe I would have wanted to be the next Wayne Gretzky myself. Instead, I wanted to be the next Michael Jordan. I wasn't the only one to admire Michael Jordan at that time. Between 1986 and 2003, kids of all races and religions, have come to admire Michael Jordan. He was and is a great role model.

When Michael Jordan entered the NBA in 1984, I was eight years old and could remember thinking to myself: "Wait a minute. This basketball thing is kind

M.J. and The Great One

of cool." In hockey, because of the equipment, the masks and the distance from the fans, you can't really see facial expressions and you definitely can't hear the players talking. It's also difficult to see the interaction between the players and the coach. But in basketball, it always intrigued me that the audience, the crowd, was allowed to get so close to the court. That, and the fact that the players seemed to interact with the crowd, whether it was diving into the front couple of rows to save a basketball, or giving 'high-fives' to members of the crowd as they're walking out onto the floor. I sat there, mesmerized by the facial expressions as Michael Jordan stood on the foul line and talked to the referee about the call. He kind of smiled and chuckled as he walked to the foul line, took a couple of dribbles, then spun the basketball. I could see him take a deep breath, exhale, flex his knees . . . then . . . he released the ball: a high arching shot with a lot of back spin. It found the bottom of the bucket. And as the ball went in, he turned to one of his teammates and spoke. I was so intrigued by the possibility of following a sport where I could actually feel like I was courtside, right by the players. The cameras would get up in the faces of the players. I could see when they were angry at the coach. I could see when they were happy with another player's performance. Or maybe they apologized to the kid in the front row for knocking his popcorn over as the loose ball flew out of control and into the crowd. All of those factors drew me to the game of basketball.

But in Brantford, the home of the hockey legend, everyone wanted to pattern their athletic careers after Wayne Gretzky. Except me. All *I* really wanted was to learn how to play basketball. It was around grade five when I made my decision to go for it. That's also when I started to experience my first taste of bullying or verbal abuse. The verbal side became clear to me when I started telling people that Michael Jordan was the man: that I wanted to be like "Mike." Wanting to be like Mike in the 80s in Brantford wasn't really popular. If you didn't want to be like Wayne, all the kids thought you were trying to "show off" or get attention.

"Why are you trying to be so different? What's so special about you? What's the big idea? You're not tough enough to play hockey?"

M.J. and The Great One

Basketball isn't a sport where you are allowed to drop the gloves and throw punches. Because of that, a lot of the kids in my class would start to tease me like this:

"Q likes to play basketball because he's not *tough* enough to play hockey. He couldn't hack the physical contact."

In the U.S., a lot of kids are into football, just as in Canada it's about hockey, or in Australia it's about rugby . . . guys who decide not to play the full-contact sports, may be teased for not "being up to the challenge." Of course, that's a major misconception.

In Brantford, when you got older and started playing junior hockey, only then you were allowed to have fist-fights, which was considered "cool." I definitely didn't see any value ever in having to drop gloves and duke it out on the ice because somebody hooked me with their stick or gave me a little body check into the boards. All of a sudden we have to drop and have a fight? That still doesn't make sense to me. The way I see it, we've been blessed with wonderful features in our human body. Our bodies are made so spectacularly, why would someone willingly sustain multiple punches or fists to the face? What is the point of repeatedly punching somebody in the face? To gain acceptance with your teammates and coach? The fans in the stands? It's so much easier to prove your differences emotionally or mentally. That's my way of thinking. But in grade five, that wasn't the norm. So I got teased a lot.

Soon, I started to come to school telling people how I wanted to become a basketball player and when I grew up, I was going to be in the NBA. How I was going to be playing right beside Michael Jordan on the Chicago Bulls. Today I'm a short white guy, but I was even shorter back then. So, you can imagine what people were thinking. Not me. I was just hoping that Jordan would still be around by the time I got my game good enough to be in the NBA. I was pretty convinced that one day Jordan and I would actually play on the same team or at very least become good friends.

I would go to school and I'd show up with Michael Jordan on my binder, with my Chicago Bulls cap and my Michael Jordan #23 basketball jersey. While I was wearing this kind of gear to school,

M.J. and The Great One

everyone else was wearing hockey jerseys and gear from the Edmonton Oilers (Gretzky's team in the 80s). So I got picked on, verbally. It was people calling me some pretty nasty names which suggested I was a "wimp" or just generally scared. You get the idea.

I can remember a particular day when I was in grade five. I was walking to school and heard a bunch of kids talking about what I had said the day before. All I had said was, "I think basketball's sweet. I think it's a cool game and I'm going to start to play real basketball." I was going to get my dad to sign me up for a league. And in the league you get your own T-shirt and your own ball.

And everybody was like, "Who cares? Whatever." They humoured me at the time and said, "Sure, that's cool."

The next day I heard a few kids starting to laugh about it. "Oh, there's Quincy. Mr. *Pro-Basketball* player. There's the Harlem Globetrotter now."

It wasn't just kids in my grade, either. The kids teasing were also in grade seven and eight. And it continued. I would walk to school with a basketball under my arm in a Michael Jordan jersey and

Q Mack

they'd start to pick on me. First it was:

"Hey, Michael Jordan! There he is! Hey, M.J.!"

I was only walking down the street, not wanting to be overly different. Sure, I wanted to play basketball but I also really wanted to fit in. I wanted everyone to like me. I don't think anyone goes out of his way to have people make fun of him. So, everyday I'd have to put up with somebody making a snide comment or taking a backhanded verbal shot at me. It would usually have something to do with basketball being "for wimps." The ones who picked on me the most were the older boys. Whatever they said, they were always implying that I was not hardcore enough to play the physical game of hockey.

A lot of times when I would get to school, people would be fooling around on the playground. Some would be playing wall ball, or marbles. Some of the girls would be skipping or playing hopscotch. I'd be dribbling a basketball and one of the older kids would come over and say: "Let me borrow that for a minute, Q." And he'd take the basketball right out of my hands. I would be standing there, absolutely powerless to do anything, and two or three grade eight

M.J. and The Great One

dudes would play a little game of "keep away." "We know how to play basketball too. Check this out, Q."

Next thing you know they're firing the ball around my head, passing it around me, setting up a game of monkey in the middle. The problem was, I wasn't really a willing participant. I hadn't asked them to come over and start the game. But that didn't stop them. The only reason they even showed up was to bug me: to taunt me about having a basketball at school.

So this "game" would go on for maybe five or ten minutes until they got bored, or until I stopped trying to get the ball back. When I stopped trying, I just sat there and said, "All right guys, when you're done playing with it, could I just have it back?"

They'd look at me and say, "Oh yeah. You can have it back. If you go get it first."

Then, one of them would do a big soccer kick and the ball would fly 50 metres into the field. I'd have to run after it while everybody laughed. Now that kind of bullying happens every day. In Canada, in the U.S., that type of playground bullying is always going on. Whether it's games of "keep away," or taking somebody's chocolate bar or drink box out of their lunch box, or making fun of somebody because they can't afford the most expensive pair of running shoes that everybody else is wearing . . . it's all the same.

It's the kids who are a little bit "different" that get excluded from the "in crowd." And it's usually that "in crowd" that runs the school. Some of them may come from a little money. Sometimes they are the best athletes in the school, or the tallest kids, or the prettiest ones. You're good at something, you dress well, you're the one with all the jokes, you're the rebel . . . whatever you do to stand out to make other people take notice usually gets you into some sort of "in crowd." And that "in crowd" is usually responsible for teasing and taunting the less fortunate kids.

In a lot of cases, the kids picked on are ones who don't have the same kind of money as everybody else. Income level varies from family to family. It always has and always will. If you're a 10 or 12 year old, it's not like you go out and buy your own pair of shoes. Maybe when you're doing the back-to-school shopping, you get the pencil crayons that cost $3.99 rather than the deluxe pencil crayons that cost

$14.99. There will be a couple kids in your class that will have the more expensive ones. And a lot of the time it's those kids who like to clown, diss, or put their noses up at the ones that just can't afford all the expensive "cool" gear. Kids whose parents just can't afford it. The kids who have the expensive shoes and the pricey backpacks and the cool hats . . . they can end up taking credit for having money that really isn't theirs. People starting to show attitude at an early age, and you know what? Adults do it, too. People bully people who don't fit into their "norm" whether it's financial, social, or physical.

From the victim's perspective, it looks like, "Why is everybody always picking on me? Why is everybody giving me a hard time? I wish I could just fit in. I wish I could slip through the cracks and not stick out so much. I just don't want everybody singling me out. I just wish somehow I could do something to get me accepted into the 'in crowd.'"

To understand bullying, it is important to look at it from not only the victim's view, but from the bully's view as well. I always wanted to be a part of the crowd that made all the jokes; that was so cool.

Q Mack

This little crowd of kids could laugh at anybody yet no one could laugh at them. In grade five, I thought, "By the time I'm in grade six, or by the time I'm in grade seven, if I could just be cool enough . . . if I could be the one tossing the jokes out instead of having the jokes tossed on me . . . then that would be the ultimate. That would be a great day in my life."

I thought this would be the sweetest deal, ever. I'd be the guy dishing out the punishments instead of being the beating post. I thought I'd just have to take my licks and pay my dues and continue to get bullied until that day when the tide would turn. There was nothing I could really do about it. When you're getting teased like that, sometimes you feel so helpless. I remember thinking to myself, "Well, I've got a couple of options here when these kids are taking my ball away. I can immediately run to the teacher and tell on them and say 'These kids are bugging me,' or I could go home to my parents and tell them the kids at school are making fun of me.'"

But we all know that complaining generally doesn't clear up a problem. Sometimes it makes it worse. When you actually go out of your way to become a tattletale, you get this in response:

"This guy can't take it. He has to go home and tell his *mommy*, or tell the principal."

We've all grown up with kids who are tattletales and it's impossible for these kids to make solid friends because people don't really want to be involved with someone who, they think, is going to tell on everything they do. And then those kids find themselves even more on the outside.

Parents and teachers always say, "If someone's bugging you, you come tell me and I'll fix it and make it all better." As much as parents or teachers want to correct a situation, at least 50% of the time they are not even present. The problem is, the adults aren't at the playground to really supervise what is going on. So going to tell somebody right away when you're being verbally bugged or teased is not always the answer. That does not include *physical bullying*, or feeling your safety is truly threatened. That, I will talk about later.

In grade six, this is what I started to do. The teasing started to become less and less when I became one of the older kids in the school. I also began

Q Mack

working on my basketball skills regardless of what anybody said to me. People kept teasing me and bugging me and saying: "Oh you think you're better than us, Quincy, because we play hockey?"

I knew I wasn't trying to be cool. I wasn't trying to show anybody up. I was just doing something that I wanted to do. Something that I really had an interest in. So, anytime somebody started bugging me about it, instead of running to "tell" on this person, I remembered what my mom always told me.

"Sticks and stones can break your bones but words can never hurt you."

When I was experiencing the bullying, it was the first time where I really understood what she meant. I thought, "At least these kids aren't using sticks and stones!" So, I let it go.

A lot of the kids on playgrounds today experience physical bullying as well. In a case of physical bullying and violence, I would fully recommend going to an authority figure. If it comes to a point where your physical safety is threatened, I'd always recommend you go to a teacher. There is absolutely no shame in bringing that to the attention of someone, whether it

M.J. and The Great One

be a teacher, principal, parent, or police officer if it gets serious enough. And there are serious situations out there.

But on the verbal side of bullying, I always thought, "Well at least these kids aren't using sticks and stones. That could be a lot more painful than just names. What's the deal with this name calling anyway?"

I really started to assess this, the best that I could at 11 years of age. "So what? These kids are calling me names? So what? These kids are starting to realize that I'm going to be a little bit different than they are and they're starting to feel uncomfortable with it. Maybe *they're* the ones starting to feel a bit threatened by the whole thing and they're trying to stand their ground."

By the time the younger kids reach grade eight, a lot of them feel they have paid their dues by taking the verbal beatings in grade five and six. So when they get to grade eight they think, "I'm going to turn around and show this kid who's running things out here on the playground."

I'm embarrassed to admit it, but I started to do

> Q Mack

exactly that as I got older, and here's why. Instead of getting sad, getting mad, getting frustrated, or being embarrassed when I was being teased, I thought, "That's cool. I'm gonna take it in stride. I'm just going to take it home and practise; the more they make fun of me, the better I'm going to get. If they think they're gonna make fun of me right now, wait for another six months or wait until next summer when they see how good I am."

I thought the better I could get at basketball, the less these kids could make fun of me. I would use basketball as a tool to make myself feel a little better. Every time these kids would beat me down verbally, I would turn it to basketball: "Okay, then . . . looks like it's time to practise the skills. Looks like it's time to try a little bit harder."

In the back of my mind, I always had the image of me walking to school one day and showing off basketball tricks or shooting a couple of half-court shots or anything cool that everybody else would find impressive. Instead of bugging me, they'd say, "Can you teach me that?" Or, "Who taught you that?" Or, "That's cool. I wish I knew how to do that."

> M.J. and The Great One

So I made it my goal to keep practising my skills until it became evident how much time I put into it. In Brantford, if you become a good hockey player, you really don't stand out. There are about 15,000 to 20,000 good hockey players in Brantford. Everybody plays hockey: boys, girls, men, women, seniors, little kids . . . everybody! There are hockey players from the age of four to seventy-four. With all those great players, you just don't stick out. But with basketball, that was a different story. So, I practised instead of letting myself get discouraged by the bullying.

But, by the time I got to grade eight, I started to participate or even ringlead a little bit in some verbal bullying operations on the playground.

I was only concerned with myself. I'd go find a couple of kids in grade five, six, seven, or even eight who looked like easy targets. Kids who appeared emotionally weaker. Kids who didn't have as much money. I always found a way to harass someone. I would gather a couple of friends around and look specifically for that kid who, I felt, was the easiest target.

I thought, "Oh, yeah. This kid's parents don't make a lot of money. He's showing up at school in

Q Mack

jogging pants with rips in them and a faded T-shirt that was a guaranteed hand-me-down. This clown really deserves to hear what I think about him."

I used to think I was special enough . . . that this kid would value my opinion, so I went over to give him a hard time. I started doing this for two or three months. At recess time, my friends and I would gather around a kid and make him do something like try to catch a football or challenge him to a race . . . anything to make this kid feel inferior and excluded from the group. I did this for a little while and we had some forced laughs about it as we'd look at how poor this kid was, or how slow, how sloppy, messy, dirty. . . . These kids would be on the receiving end of verbal abuse from me. Now it was *me* calling them names, making fun of them.

I realized though, around Christmas time, that what I was doing was not cool. "This isn't even close to cool," I thought. "This is exactly how I used to feel every day when I walked home. I'd be thinking about the older kids and their voices would be ringing in my ears and . . . this is terrible! This is exactly what those

M.J. and The Great One

kids did to me! Now, three or four years later, here I stand, just because I got a little better at basketball, because I grew a couple of inches, or am a little bit stronger than before, now I think I have the right? This is bogus, man."

I thought it was my duty to become the class clown: to do whatever it took to get a laugh. The easiest laughs were always the easiest targets, and to me that's not good comedy. That's cheap laughter. So I'm getting these kids to laugh by harassing this poor kid who can't afford to buy the T-shirt that I'm wearing? Or picking on this kid who doesn't know anything about basketball or hockey and doesn't even like sports by calling him the "ultimate wimp"?

I started thinking to myself, "This is crazy. Q, what are you doing? This is what those kids did to you. And how did *you* feel about it?" Well, I knew exactly how I felt about it. My confidence level went way down. I started thinking to myself, "You know what? Maybe the bullies are right." Some kids even started to believe the garbage that's being spouted at them: "You're no good. You're too short. You're too slow. You suck."

> Q Mack

Anybody can get a laugh using an easy target. Only the truly funny and creative individuals do not need to bring someone down in order to put themselves up. If you have to drag someone down through the mud to make yourself look better, then that's using someone else as a stepping stone. If I have to make jokes about somebody's bad hair days, or lack of funds to make myself feel better, then that proves that I am the one with the low self-confidence. The people who feel that it's their duty to bully or harass other kids are usually the ones who themselves are hurting the most.

If you ask your entire student body who the "bullies" in school are, you'll get a few names in common. Even in grade one or two there are a couple of people who get into the verbal abuse. If they start to make fun of everybody else, no one will make fun of *them*. They want to distract people from their own shortcomings.

If you're reading this book right now, and you're one of those kids who thinks it's cool to make fun of other people or physically pick on someone else and you truly believe that it is okay, I, Q Mack, feel sorry

M.J. and The Great One

for you because that's an immature attitude. Roll your eyes if you want to, because when I was in grade seven, I would have probably rolled my eyes too.

"Yeah, whatever man," I'd think. "You don't understand. You don't know how it is."

The fact of the matter is, I do understand. I do know how it is. I was there. Trust me, I know how you feel because I felt the same way. But you know what I found? It does not have to be like that. You never have to clown somebody else to build yourself up. The best way to build yourself up is find a positive way to build your confidence level. I'll give you a couple ways to get your confidence level going through the roof in our next chapter.

I was a part of the cycle of bullying. I was a victim. I was an offender. And now, standing back from the situation, I still see victims every day, kids and adults included. I see people who are bullies, kids and adults alike. I encourage you to break this cycle. I don't care who you think is cool. I don't care who told you that fist fighting is the way to solve your problems. I'm telling you right now that it's not. It's only going to land you in trouble, get you hurt.

> Mack

I know a kid I went to high school with who was always a tough guy. If he heard you had been talking about him, or if you looked at him wrong, he'd always confront you. He'd push you against the locker, grab you by the shirt, knock the books out of your hands, or challenge you to a fist fight. He *always* wanted to fight.

A couple of years after we were done high school, the same kid — who was not much of a kid anymore — had the same attitude. He still had this immature desire to fight people as a way of settling his problems. One night, at a club, he got into a confrontation with another dude. It was a meaningless argument being spewed back and forth. And of course, the guy I knew said, "Let's take this out to the parking lot, buddy."

So they did. The fist fight started, and the guy I knew from high school punched the smaller dude a couple of times in the face. There was a crowd of people standing around them like a group of idiots, chanting "FIGHT FIGHT FIGHT!" Nobody made an effort to break it up. The smaller dude crumpled. As he fell, he struck his forehead against the curb . . . and he died. Dead.

M.J. and The Great One

It's harsh to read about, and I apologize if it's a little startling but it's true. The guy fell to the sidewalk that night and died. What do you think the young guy's parents thought? What about his little brother or sister? What do you think his friends thought as they imagined him crumpled on the sidewalk . . . dead? Did they think, "Man, that guy's a tough fighter." Or, "Wow, what a tough guy he is," or "At least he was standing up for himself"?

No. They think, "What a shame. What an immature move. What an unfortunate move. What a bad decision. What a ridiculous incident and what an avoidable situation this was."

Physical confrontations never solve anything. The fact is, they usually start with verbal bullying, taunting, teasing, and harassment. Nothing positive comes out of physical violence. Usually you're left with more confusion, and more anger.

I was harassed in grade five. Then, in grade eight, I thought, "Perfect. It's my time to do the harassing." Midway through I realized it was a stupid move. *It felt bad to get bullied and didn't feel much better to be on the other side of that spectrum either.*

Q Mack

Nothing cool about that. *Everyone is a victim of bullying, even the bullies themselves.* So solve the problem by breaking the cycle. It's your choice.

The Correct Formula   10

 Somebody becomes a bully because they don't feel very good about themselves. But bullying doesn't solve the problem. The solution is confidence building, making sure that you never have to find yourself in a situation where you feel so low and insecure that you have to start putting other people down either physically or verbally to feel better.

Perhaps your confidence level is beginning to slip or perhaps you don't think much of yourself. Maybe you're insecure, maybe

Q Mack

you're shy. Here are the top five ways to boost your confidence. Confidence level is the single most important element to achieve success of any kind. Without it your boat has already gone the way of the Titanic before you even get a chance to pull out of the dock. Without a higher confidence level, how can you begin to achieve a goal? Perhaps you want to meet new people, but if you feel low about yourself you probably wouldn't even attempt to begin to speak to someone new because you would be worried that it might turn out poorly. Perhaps you think you won't know what to say or it will backfire. You might think things aren't going to work out well for you, so instead of having it get worse, you just stop trying. So, first things first. Boost your confidence.

These are the five ways that I have found help boost my own confidence level. Whenever I felt I was lacking skills in some areas, like public speaking, or I was worried about doing something brand new such as writing a business plan, these are five things I put into practice in order to bolster my confidence level.

The Correct Formula

- *Dare to be different.*
- *Attempt new things.*
- *Find out what you are good at.*
- *Admit and address your weaknesses.*
- *Place yourself in pressure situations of various degrees.*

Daring to be different is a great way to boost your confidence. Now, the word "different" doesn't necessarily mean "freaky" or "outcast." When people hear the word "different," they may think:

"Oh, man. I don't want to be *too* different. I don't want to be so different that people won't accept me. I don't want to be so different in the way that I talk or act or walk or dress or behave that people will think I'm an outcast or a freak."

This is not about impressing other people or making an extreme statement. It's about being comfortable with yourself. You've got to find a way to be comfortable with yourself. And one of the best ways to quickly be comfortable with yourself is to start accepting you . . . for you. Daring to be different means actually having the guts to improve on your personal situation. It takes a lot of intestinal fortitude to go out of your way to improve yourself. That could mean asking the teacher for a little bit of extra help on a subject. Or if you're on a sports team in high school, perhaps renting a couple of instructional videos or approaching an older player who has more experience and asking for some tips so that you can improve your own game.

Myself? I head to the bookstore to read about other people in my field. I'm encouraged and often enlightened when I read about individuals who have gone through the same struggles that I am currently going through. For me, I'm trying to become a better businessman and basketball trickster. For you it might be a better math student. That's why asking questions helps you in not only improving your skill, but bolstering your confidence level.

The word "confidence" means to have a sense of "self-reliance" or "boldness." It's about believing in

The Correct Formula

yourself. For example, I'm very confident in my hands right now. I fully trust my hand/eye coordination. I know that if I throw an apple behind my back, I can reach back and catch it without looking at it. I'm very confident that I can stand with my back towards the basket, throw the ball over my shoulder and make that shot. I'm confident of things like that only because I dared to be different enough to put myself in that situation. I continued to practise and become better at something that maybe not everybody else saw the value in. Not everybody else sees the value of becoming a better student or a better basketball player or a better brother/sister or friend. That in itself may be daring to be different because it is something you are doing that is about you, and no one else.

When everybody else is at a wild party on Saturday night, you have a choice. You can think, "Do I do it up with everybody else tonight just so everybody won't think I'm goofy or strange? Do I just do what everybody else is doing just to fit in?"

Well? Do you dare to be different? Or are you going to strive to be the same and do what everybody else is doing even if it isn't what you want to do. It may even make you uncomfortable. There's a certain path that most people take, and there's nothing wrong with that. But just because everybody takes that route, doesn't mean that *you* have to do that.

There's nothing more dangerous than following a pattern because it's the "easy" thing to do. I would recommend doing a little bit of research on your own. Find out about different career paths or sports or courses in school or places to travel to around the world. Do your own research. Don't let someone else's research dictate the direction you choose to take in life.

Also, don't let the rate of speed it takes for you to accomplish something be dictated by your sister or brother's accomplishments. Okay, so your older brother may have been riding a bicycle by the time he was five years old. That doesn't mean you have to be on the exact same path. It doesn't really matter what anybody else is doing. It only matters that you are doing the best that you can do. Your best isn't your brother's best or your best friend's best. *Your* best is *your* best. And as long as you are honest with yourself.

The Correct Formula

It's okay to say, "Hey, I'm daring to be a little bit different. I choose to control what rate of speed I'm going to go at. I'm going to choose what's right for me."

If you're in class right now, I'm not suggesting you start thinking, "Doesn't matter what the teacher says about math or spelling, I'm going to decide how fast I learn this, or how fast this project or test gets done."

That's not what I'm talking about. When you're working inside of a system like school or a job, you don't just decide what time you're going to roll in to work. If you've been hired to work at a law firm for $100,000 a year, you don't just *decide* that you're not going to show up on Monday morning. When you're working inside of a system, there are rules. If you're on a basketball team and the coach tells you that you're running a certain play, you don't say:

"Well, I'm not going to let somebody else dictate what play I'm going to run. I'm going to run whatever play I want to."

What I'm talking about applies to your free time. What are you going to do with your free time? Are you going to sit and play video games for six hours or read and learn some new things? That's totally up to you. That's when I dare you to be a little different. When you have some free time, do something different with it. Find something that you'd like to try. Get creative.

I always wanted to look a little bit different from everyone else. I would do something unusual with my hair and people would come up to me: "Wow, who did that for you? That's pretty sweet."

And the next thing you know I was talking to somebody who I wouldn't normally have spoken with. That was different. I always found ways to stand out — whether it was cutting the brim off my baseball hat or getting a crazy haircut or flipping up my shades or having a couple of crazy jokes — whatever it was, it was something that was a little bit daring and a little bit different. When you let go of any concern regarding possible comments you may get from others, you get accustomed and comfortable with yourself. That brings your confidence level up. It doesn't really matter what a person thinks about my appearance so long as I feel comfortable with what I've got going on. When you feel comfort-

The Correct Formula

able with yourself other people recognize that and start to feel comfortable with you. So, do you dare?

Attempt new things. Get out of your comfort zone. So many people stay inside their comfort zone and never explore new possibilities. "Well, I'm good at this and I'm good at that and so why bother with anything else?"

Why? Why not! It's very difficult to boost your confidence if you do the same thing you've always done. It's the constant change that encourages or bolsters confidence levels. It's very easy to get into a comfort zone and say, "Why fix it if it ain't broke?" I think too many people lose sight of the fact that nothing feels better than boosting your confidence. After all, it is a human reaction to avoid change. In fact, in North America, one of the largest fears among individuals is "change."

By attempting new things, you get a great sense of accomplishment. Think about it. How will you know if you like something, or are good at something if you never try it? It's like adding to your bag of tricks or increasing your repertoire. If I looked at every new basketball trick and said, "Forget that, who cares? Not really important anyway," rather than attempting it, then I'm really missing out on some extra confidence that I could have received if I had just taken that trick and given it a whirl.

Let's say I was at a Japanese restaurant and a friend ordered sushi and asked if I wanted to try some and I said, "Naw, forget it. I've never tried sushi before, but I probably won't like it so I'm not going to bother." I just missed out on that little boost of confidence that I could have received if I would have tried it. By trying it, I'm saying, "Hey, I've got the courage to do something outside of my 'comfort zone.' Cool!"

If you try something new and you don't like it, what's the loss? That's what it comes down to. If you like it, add it to the repertoire. If you don't like it then you can honestly say you've tried it. Okay, so you didn't necessarily like it, but at least now you know.

Remember this quote: "If you always do what you've always done then you'll always get what you've always got."

If you keep doing things the way you've always

The Correct Formula

done them, then you're going to keep getting what you've always got. If you've got 65% in a subject and you keep studying the way you've always studied, then you'll keep getting that same mark. *If you want to step things up in life, whether it be in school or in your personal life, then hey — change your ways. Don't be afraid of change.*

When you dare to be different and you try new things, you really start to *find out what you're good at.* And when you find out what you're good at, that is when things really start to come together. Because one of the greatest motivators in life is knowing that you're *good* at something. When you're good at something you start to gain recognition, whether it is from your peers or coaches, teachers or parents . . . when you're good at something people start to notice and that feels great. And when you find out what you're good at, that is fantastic because you can get even better at it.

Let's say you have never played baseball before. And let's say a friend of yours suggests you get into a game with some friends. Then, suddenly, you're up

Q Mack

to bat and you're hitting the ball hard and far. You'd be thinking:

"Wow, I'm kind of good at this even though I've never tried it before. It was a pretty daring move to get into this game. I'm not a baseball player. I've never really done the baseball thing before but my friend said I might be good at it. I wasn't really sure but I attempted something brand new and hey, I'm actually good at it."

And you keep hitting the ball far into the field. All of your friends might be saying, "Wow! I can't believe it. This guy is so good! I can't believe how talented this guy is. He's a natural! A natural! This guy's fantastic!" What do you think that does for your confidence level?

Now you may have got onto that field and thought, "Oooh. This isn't really for me. I don't think this is going anywhere. I don't think I've got a future in baseball. It's not really working out."

Hey, that's okay. People will respect that you were willing to try it. You were willing to give a run and if you didn't like it, so, what's the loss? At least you know now that you don't like it. Now you can try something else.

The Correct Formula

When you find out what you're good at, you have the ability and the motivation to get better at it. My dad always gave me this career advice: *"Find what it is you're really good at and then get so good at it that people want to start paying you to do it."*

Take a look at a comedian, an actor, an athlete, a musician — somebody that you look up to as having exceptional skill in some area. This person could be a magician, a D.J., a lawyer, a hypnotist, or a dancer. It's pretty common to think, "I wonder how he or she got so *good* at that." I always hear people saying, "That singer was an overnight success," or, "This athlete is an overnight sensation." Let me tell you, there's nothing "overnight" about any of those successes. That process started years and years in advance.

When people find out what they're good at, they have the added confidence to really improve and maximize their potential in that area. You have to pinpoint what it is that you are good at so you can use your energy to get even better.

Now, once you've dared to be different by attempting new things, soon you'll find out what you're good at. Then, once you find out what you're good at, you'll also find out what you're not good at. That means you can *admit and address your weaknesses.* It's important to know where your talents lie, but equally important is knowing your weaknesses.

When you discover what you're not so good at, you have a couple of options.

1) You can put it to one side and not touch it with a 10-foot pole.
2) You can start working selectively to get better in those areas.

I believe there are certain life skills that everybody needs to work on. Sometimes daily. The first involves learning to effectively communicate with other people. You don't have to be an extreme "people person" to do this. Everybody needs to improve his or her communication techniques — even people such as myself who speak and communicate with people for a living. This is what I do: I speak, I communicate, I relate, I connect, I discuss. It doesn't matter how good you are, you can always stand to get better. You

The Correct Formula

can always improve. You can always get better tomorrow than you were today with a bit of preparation and practice. Communication is how we relate to each other as human beings. If you aren't communicating well with someone, ask yourself why? Put yourself in their shoes. How do you think they are interpreting what you say? There are many ways to improve communication and they're out there for you to find.

There are also certain skills you'll learn at school that are extremely important. Some skills you'll be better at than others. That doesn't mean you shouldn't pay attention to the ones you aren't as good at. To admit and address your weaknesses is key. Remember, no one is perfect. It's usually the people who think that they're perfect that have a little bit more self-examination to do. Everyone has areas they need to work on or improve on.

So what do you do if you have an area, in school for example, that you're not so good at?

Ask for help.

I know there are a few things that I'm really good at. In fact, there are a few things I'm *great* at. I'm a

> Q Mack

great basketball trickster. I'm a skillful communicator. I'm a quality entertainer. I'm pretty good at being a team leader. As a speaker, I also do pretty well. But after those four or five things, my list begins to trail off quite significantly. In fact, I could probably name 25 things that I do rather poorly. People only get to see the things that I do really well. Why? Because I do the things that I'm good at as much as possible. When it comes to the things that I'm not so good at, well that's when I ask for help.

When it comes to my company, I search out the best candidate to complement my strengths by making sure they compensate for some of my weaknesses. For example, I knew when I started this business that I needed someone to handle the "business" side of things. When I began, it was a very small type of operation where I performed in about 100 schools my first year. There was no website or video or products to be sold. It was strictly, "Sign me up to come to your school, I'll do a little show and then I'm out of there." I could communicate and entertain and do the three or four things I'm good at on a daily basis.

The Correct Formula

But when I went from 100 schools to 200 in both Ontario and the U.S., I had to start thinking a little bit bigger. I know I'm not an administrator. I'm also not very good at following through with many minor but important details. I'm known to overlook notes left on desks and I'm not very good at returning phone calls and staying on schedule. I've got so many things on my plate at one time that I need someone who can help me organize my weaknesses.

There were about ten things that I needed in order to run a successful business. Of the ten, I knew I could complete about three of them. Three out of ten. Well, a business does not run with one person. What I needed was a little bit of help. I had admitted and addressed my own weaknesses, so I needed to hire someone around my shortcomings. Why would I hire somebody who is an entertainer or a master communicator? I can already do those things. I needed somebody who could set up a data base. I needed somebody who could help with the year-end accounting and somebody who could help me return phone calls and schedule my year efficiently. I needed

Q Mack

people who could complement me: a real team.

A good team has players who are talented in different things. You don't want a team full of forwards. You need some guards in there, along with a few key shooters. *One person's weakness is often another's strength.* Maybe you're great at English, but terrible at math. That doesn't mean you can delegate your math homework to your friend who happens to be great with numbers. Instead, what if your friend helps you practise? Maybe you can help another friend with his or her English skills. That way, you each use your strengths to help one another improve on your weaknesses. I had no problem admitting and addressing my weaknesses. When you can do that, then you can really move ahead. The more you ask for help, the more you can improve. And that boosts your confidence level.

You've been gaining confidence from daring to be different, and attempting new things. Now, you've found out what you're good at and can admit and address your weaknesses. So it's time to start using this confidence by *placing yourself in pressure situa-*

The Correct Formula

tions of varying degrees to see how far this confidence is going to carry you.

Imagine you're playing a video game with ten levels of difficulty. You've finally unlocked the door to level number three. Now, you've already completed levels one and two a few times so you feel comfortable with them. Then, you manage to complete level three. Now you're starting to feel confident about the first *three* levels. The next step is using that gained confidence to step up to level number four. You have to keep progressing. Your only choice is to keep placing yourself in pressure situations where you must perform; otherwise you just pack it up, shut down, and go home.

The only choice I present myself with is this:

"Well, Q . . . You can get up on stage here in front of these 10,000 people, turn your microphone on, and do what you do best, or you can shut your microphone off, take your basketball, get in your car, and drive away from this place and pretend nothing happened."

Those are the two choices. *You can perform, or you can choose to run away. The key is to use that confidence level to your advantage.* You now know what you do well. Put that confidence to use and put yourself into a pressure situation. Get up in front of a group of people and speak, or put your hand up to answer that question in class. Volunteer to read out loud. Do what you have to do to put yourself in pressure situations.

Sometimes situations can be a little bit more challenging than others but that's cool. You don't have to toss yourself onto the floor of the Air Canada Centre tomorrow or run for Prime Minister of Canada or the President of the U.S. No one's asking you to jump up seven or eight different steps in one go. But hey, find little ways every day to use your growing confidence level.

First, you've got to dare to be different and attempt new things. Then, you'll find out what you're good at and what your weaknesses are. Finally, knowing all of that, place yourself in different pressure situations. Test your new confidence and continually improve. That's all it takes.

So what are you waiting for?

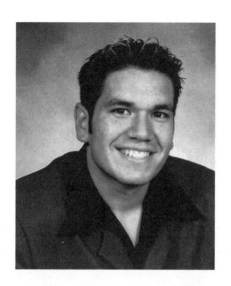

"It's Showtime, Baby!"

Near the end of high school, I realized very quickly that I wasn't going to make the NBA. I was a five-foot 10" dude and only an average athlete; therefore I wasn't an NBA prospect. After grade 13, if you weren't going to play college or university basketball you just went on with your life. For years, basketball had been such a major portion of my life, and even though I wasn't going to play basketball in college or university, I still wanted to play every single day. At first I considered coaching but I didn't take that

> Q Mack

route. Instead, I looked at basketball from a different perspective. I realized that this was where I could start making my own rules. Every basketball game I'd ever played in my life up to that point was very structured. We'd practise at a specific time, and go through specific drills. In grade 13, I realized I could finally take control of the situation. I planned out how I was going to allot my practice time now that I would be going into the gym by myself.

I kept practising basketball tricks, even though I couldn't see how I was going to achieve my final goal. It always stayed in the back of my head. While working up to that, however, I needed to get a job. I always made sure to go for jobs that would allow me to grow further in the direction I was heading in. I was a camp counsellor for awhile, as well as a camp athletics director. I was open to anything so long as I could work with kids, or teach a skill. It could be basketball, it could be arts and crafts. I didn't mind.

One job I had involved teaching clinics at summer basketball camps. I'd do a 30- to 40-minute talk on basketball tricks or shooting. I'd teach around 200 kids to shoot the basketball properly. The basketball

"It's Showtime, Baby!"

element was fun, of course, but it was the public speaking that I really liked. That was what pushed me into the radio broadcasting field. At the end of high school, I had decided to go for the Humber College radio broadcasting program. I loved the idea of being on the radio. I thought it would be the coolest to have a radio job.

In my first year at Humber College I spent many hours in the gym while the basketball team practised. The coach and other players wondered why I wasn't on the team. "You're a good shooter. I can't believe you're not on the team."

I didn't have the heart to tell the coach that I didn't care about playing competitive basketball anymore. It wasn't my dream. My dream was to work with the Raptors and Nike as a professional basketball trickster. My dream was to be my own boss and create something that would include the interests that I developed as a kid. When I was 12, all the things that were "supposed" to appeal to us just went through one ear and out the other. Some guy might come into my school with a banjo and a kazoo and some balloons to twist, and tell us: "This is a pterodactyl. He

> Q Mack

doesn't fight with the monkey. Look at that." I'd think, "What, are you kidding me?" Sure, I got what he was saying, but I wasn't buying into it.

When I was a kid, I wanted somebody to stimulate my mind. I decided that if I could create something I would have wanted to see as a kid, then that would be cool. The concept for a motivational show didn't materialize until I was 24, however. There were five years where it stayed in the back of my mind and I kept practising towards it. I spent that time thinking, "How can I get this in front of schools? How can I get in front of Nike?"

When I graduated from Humber College, I made my way to get a real job in radio. I started working at a community station just outside of Brantford. I was so happy that I was able to get a job straight out of school. My program had only lasted two years. I was out of school at 21. The only problem was, all my friends were still completing their four-year programs in university. I still wanted to live the college life with my friends. So I thought, I'll move to Guelph and work with the university basketball team. I ended up working as the announcer for the team as well as

> "It's Showtime, Baby!"

doing some radio work for Rogers. It was great to be involved in basketball again.

At the University of Guelph, I was the man with the mic. Being the centre court announcer was sweet seeing as a lot of my best friends played on the basketball teams — girls and guys. I'd sit there and get to announce my friends: "And now . . . from Montreal, number 21 in the program, number one in your hearts . . . Charles . . . YEARWOOD!"

And out came my close friend Chuck Yearwood. Chuck played for five years on the University of Guelph team. When he graduated, he went on to work with Nike Canada in the sports marketing department. Chuck first approached me about working with the company in the summer of 1997. He had only been working at Nike for a couple of months.

"We do this thing called the National NBA Hoop It Up Tour," he told me.

"What's that all about?" I asked.

"You know that three-on-three summer basketball tournament that travels across Canada?"

"Oh, yeah. I played in that as a kid. In Toronto."

> Q Mack

"That's the one," he said.

In the summer, Nike sets up an interactive court called the "Sports Court." This year it was called the "Nike Cage." It's a big rubberized court with stands around the sides where thousands of spectators can check out the action all day.

Chuck said, "We have an opening for an MC on the court. The MC gets a microphone and his job is to keep the court running for about seven or eight hours on Saturday and then again on Sunday. Do you think you could handle it?"

Even though I wasn't sure, I said with a straight face, "Oh yeah, count me in. I am the guy. Make me the guy."

I could not let this opportunity pass. Every year there's an NBA player at the event. I thought, "Man, with NBA guys around here and all these Nike representatives hanging around, this is a great time for networking. Even if I'm scared, even if I screw up. Even if I'm not as good as I want people to think that I am, it doesn't matter. I'm going for it."

The job itself consisted of showing up at the court at 8:00 a.m. From nine to five, I got to play

"It's Showtime, Baby!"

interactive games with the kids. About 3000 kids would line up to play at my court. We travelled across Canada to London, Toronto, Vancouver, and Montreal. It was one of those experiences where I had to learn as I went along.

People loved what I did. Not only did Nike have an MC who could really use the mic, but they finally had someone who could do tricks at the same time. That was key. They didn't want the MC to just stand there like a game show host. It was much better to have an individual who could *show* the kids what to do. After seeing the job I was doing, Nike said, "We want you to do this every year you're available."

By 2000, I spoke to Chuck about my idea for a school show.

"You've got to be a little more solid about your idea if Nike is going to get involved with it," he said.

Nike's the largest sports marketing company in the world. The Nike swoosh is one of the most recognizable symbols, period. So they don't mess around with somebody who says, "Hey, I have this neat idea." Everybody approaches Nike wanting something. Nike has 60 to 70 requests on a weekly basis for

Q Mack

sponsorship, and that's just in Ontario. So, I was just laying low thinking, "If Nike could get on board with this, the Nike swoosh would give me credibility with the people who don't know who I am."

Nike wouldn't sponsor anything that they would be ashamed of. So I thought, "Okay, I need to create a show. I need to bring them something. I won't just give them an idea but prove to them that I have something here. I need to get 100 schools that want to see me." So I wrote different story lines and linked tricks. Then I approached Nike.

And Nike said: "How solid is this presentation?"

"Well it's sixty minutes long. I've booked up my 100 schools. I sent out about 500 information packets," I told them.

The information packet consisted of a page talking about the show I was going to do. I intended to talk about confidence building, goal setting, and positive attitude. At the show, I was going to give out some Nike prizes. I bought prizes through Chuck after telling him what I was going to do. The people at his work started asking him, "Chuck, that's a big box of gear you're taking out of the office. Who's it for?"

"It's Showtime, Baby!"

And Chuck told them, "It's for Quincy, our MC from Hoop It Up. He's doing this school thing." So Chuck started to get people warm to the idea from the inside. From there the idea moved pretty quickly.

Nike told me: "Do this year's tour and let us know what your success rate is. We want feedback. We want to know what the principals thought. Get us some letters."

So that's what I did. I went for a year without being sponsored, buying the prizes and gear myself. That summer, I worked at Hoop It Up again, and my responsibilities grew. Our court had all the action. I'd pull out a pair of Nike shoes and tell the crowd:

"Whoever can shoot the ball in first can have these sweet shoes. Oh, did I mention you have to shoot the ball like this?"

Then, I'd shoot the ball over my head, show them how it's done, and the crowd would go wild.

I'd say, "Hey you can do it, it's not so hard."

Then I'd shoot it again. We'd go through a zigzag line-up of 400 kids. I'd bring out more shoes, telling them I now had *five* pairs to give away before five o'clock. My first year I had to ask when I could give out

> Q Mack

gear. At this point, I was able to run the show my way.

The NBA reps also have a court at Hoop It Up called the NBA Center Court. They started coming over to me and saying,

"Hey Q, can you MC our dunk contest while you're on your break? At the Nike court, you have the whole place rocking."

The NBA guys had noticed that our court had some real hype. So I took the opportunity in hand.

"Okay, but it's gonna cost you," I said. "I won't charge you money. And I won't just MC in London. I'll do it for you in Montreal, in Toronto, and in Vancouver. I'll work an extra two hours a day. I'll do it for Raptors tickets. My mom would really love to go to a Raptors game this year. In fact, I'd like to go to a few myself."

"No problem," they said.

The first time I ever performed professionally, it was incredible. I had been visualizing the show for three or four weeks. Now, I just had to bring the goods. At the Grand Woodland School in Brantford, I stood up on the stage and thought: "Oh yeah, I've already been here, in my mind anyway."

> "It's Showtime, Baby!"

It was just as I had imagined. I looked out at the 275 students and the 20 teachers and realized I wasn't nervous. I was really excited. That first day, I didn't want to mess up in any way or let anybody down. I just wanted to deliver what I promised. And in my head, the first thought was, "Can you? Can you do it?"

"Yes," I thought. "Just do what you do well."

I couldn't believe that if this worked out, I would be able to do it every day.

Communication and basketball are the two things I love most in the world. I get to do them every day. Overnight success? No way. I've been practising for fifteen years. One of the biggest motivating factors in life is finding something you're good at doing. Dream, visualize, practise, explore opportunities including challenging ones and don't lose hope.

What's up next for me?

I operate a summer basketball camp called the SHOWTIME ACADEMY. Check out QMack.com for more details. Come see me at Hoop It Up this summer. Watch for me on major TV stations and sports networks.

Q Mack

Talking about following your dreams, let me tell you about Jeremy Knot. Jeremy is from Thorloe, Ontario, about five hours north of North Bay. He's an 18-year-old beat boxer. He can make the sound of any drum machine with his mouth. He is a first-class talent. He's been practising beat boxing for the last eight years in a country music town where *nobody* likes rap. Everyone keeps asking him why he's bothering to do this? He didn't get a lot of support from his friends and family, but he continued to perfect his talent and now he's getting his big break.

I met him while working in the Nike tent at an OFSAA track and field event in summertime in Belleville, 2002. I was doing a three-hour performance, and while I was doing it, I gave an open call on the mic asking if anybody wanted to come up and perform a trick with me, or do some clean freestyle rap with the mic. A lot of people can rap, but nobody I've ever met can beat box like this.

He came up to me and said, "Q, I don't rap."

"What do you do?"

"I beat box," he said.

Well, I wasn't just going to hand over the micro-

> "It's Showtime, Baby!"

phone without getting an idea of what this kid could do.

So I said, "Listen kid why don't you beat box in my ear for 30 seconds and then I'll hand over the mic."

I was absolutely astounded. I reorganized the show for the last ten minutes just so people could hear this kid. Chuck Yearwood was the featured DJ, so I told him to spin something for 30 seconds. Then, I told the crowd, "I want my friend here, 'J. Spice' (the name I came up with) to battle your sound *only* with his mouth."

So Chuck started going for thirty seconds and then everyone applauded.

So I said, "Okay, J. Let's do it."

The crowd was silent. All the adults were shocked. Everybody thought it was some kind of joke and a CD was actually playing in the background.

This guy is in his own league. He's a world class talent. The best part about it is he doesn't need a microphone, or any special props. He's that good. He'll make your head explode in 60 seconds. I'm pretty cocky. It takes a lot to impress me. I'm also a

> Q Mack

pretty good judge of talent. This kid is going to be huge and he's still in high school. He's following his dreams. So it doesn't matter what age you are. Start now. Start when you're young. Anything is possible.

Who knows? If you practise hard and perfect your talent I may come looking for you!

The Little Known FA**Q**

1 **Q will host an upcoming Saturday morning show for kids.**

By fall of 2003 you can expect to see a Saturday morning children's show hosted by yours truly. It's half an hour long and a little bit like the show "NBA Inside Stuff." We'll have a couple guests every week. The guest list could include Tiger Woods, Vince Carter, Michael Jordan, Ja Rule and J. Lo, but you'll have to stay tuned to be sure. Every week we have a comfortable interview session with that guest. We'll have the freestyle trick of the week where I teach the viewers a new trick. Also, we'll do some NBA highlights and Raptor buzz, and a sweet video-game session.

Q Mack

2   Q talks to himself out loud during practice sessions.

Constantly! People in the gym think it's kind of weird. I usually have a serious practice session of three to five hours. Every time I get the gym, I figure I might as well be in there for the long haul. By hour number two I'm getting into some serious trick sessions. Maybe I'll try to shoot the over-my-head on a half-court shot . . . 150 times. When I'm talking, most of the time I'm encouraging myself. Sometimes I reprimand myself. I'll say things like:

"C'mon Q, you knew you had to throw it higher than that! Go easy on this."

After shooting the shot: "More backspin. C'mon Q, you're better than that. Now, relax."

Now other people in the gym are looking at me thinking, "Is this guy talking to me?"

"Power's good, but let's get this together. . . . C'mon baby, you've got more in you than this!"

I talk to myself as if I was a coach. What would I be saying if I was training a kid? I never talk to myself out loud in every day life. Just during practice.

The Little Known FAQ

3 **Q can throw a football almost 45 yards — behind his back!**

True. It started with Mrs. Riimand, my grade seven and eight gym teacher. She was the one who inspired me to learn these crazy tricks. I was so jealous of the things she could do with her hands. She could juggle, throw a Frisbee like a baseball, and throw a football behind her back. I was 12 years old and jealous that she could do everything better than me. I was one of the best athletes in my school at the time, and I got pushed by my friends to step up and challenge her. Every time, she'd beat me. I was embarrassed that this teacher could do everything better than me. So, I learned how to throw a football behind my back because she could. My football trick, thanks to Shelley Riimand, involves me throwing a football 45 yards behind my back. I learned it because I didn't want to get shown up every day.

Q Mack

4   Q is totally freaked out by sharks.

Totally. My Director of Operations, Scott McNab, talks about performing shows in Australia. He thinks it's a good idea for the international exposure, but he also wants to surf. I always tell him I'll perform in California, Florida, Australia . . . anywhere where there are sharks off the coast. But I do have a problem entering the water. If there's even a chance that a small shark will be close to the shore, I'm on land. I'm at the cabana or in the pool. I got really freaked out when I saw the movie *Jaws* as a kid. We have a pool at home and sometimes, as kids, we'd scare ourselves by watching *Jaws* then going out to the pool, shutting the lights off and seeing who was too scared to jump into the dark water. Not good. When I got older I started watching "Shark Week" on the Discovery Channel. It's five days of the craziest shark footage you've ever seen. The human world is *on land*. When humans go into the water, they go for entertainment. You can find a lot of entertainment on land and not invade somebody else's world. I'm great in pools and in lakes, but when it comes to oceans, I get a little bit freaked out.

5 — Q loves to eat "old school" candy.

I eat the old school candy. I know convenience stores like 7/11 and Beckers inside out. I can maximize a $20 bill like no one else. The old school candy I'm talking about includes Popeye candy sticks, Fun Dip, Cotton Candy, Pez, Thrills gum, Mike and Ikes Hot Tamales, Big Gummy Feet, Hot Lips, the mini marshmallow strawberries and bananas, Gold Rush yellow gum nuggets. . . . I'm not big into chocolate bars. I'm not big into chips. I don't like burgers and fries or pop. My downfall is sugary candy. I love sponge toffee and peanut brittle. I like maple sugar shaped in maple leaves. I love candy bracelets and ring pops. Those are the bomb. I'm a candy freak. I've also had a few cavities in my day. Just a reminder: brush your teeth before you sleep. You don't want eight hours of sugar sitting on your teeth. I've got the cavities to prove it.

Q Mack

6 — Q drives over 15,000 km a month.

In order to get to these shows, I drive. Some of these schools are spread out as far north as Ottawa and as far south as Orlando, Florida. We're going to be in San Francisco this year. I have performed in Kentucky, Ohio, New York City, and all over Ontario. There are mornings where I have to drive to perform two shows in Windsor that same day. The alarm goes off at 4:10 a.m. and I have to get going because I have to be on the road at 4:30 in order to get there for 8:00 a.m. I drive a minimum of 300 km per day just going from Guelph to my office in Richmond Hill. When I went to Florida, it was close to 7000 km there and back. Driving is a big part of the job. In a year, I'm doing about 200,000 km. I can now navigate my way around in over 500 cities by myself. It's cool to be able to know a lot of cities. Soon, I'll have a new vehicle with a navigational system in it, which will be very sweet. I might even hook up a PlayStation 2 for additional entertainment.

The Little Known FA**Q**

7 **Q has worn Nike gear exclusively since 1990.**

Even since 1988, I've been into Michael Jordan. Whatever he did, I was down with it. He was the best, so I wanted to be the best. He still is the best. Why would I want to wear something the second best guy wears? I had nothing against other labels, but why would I want to wear anything but the best when I want to be the best? So I started saving up my birthday money, allowances, everything... to buy Air Jordans. I asked for Nike T-shirts, Michael Jordan hats... I just wanted to dress like Michael Jordan. My first day of grade nine I was wearing the Nike Air Jordan's number three. I had a red Nike shirt on. I had a silent allegiance to Nike. Being sponsored by Nike right now is no surprise to me. I wanted to be with the number one sports marketer in the world. I wanted to be the best like Michael Jordan. Nike supports my efforts to be the best. Their motto is maximum participation for all athletes. They provide me with the gear to maximize my performance. I've been paying Nike to be their billboard for the last ten years. Now they want to give it to me for free. No problem! Help yourself, and others will help you.

8 Q shaves his legs.

If you get close enough to me, you'll notice that like many other athletes, I shave my legs. Lots of cyclists, basketball players, swimmers all do it for practical reasons. When I was in grade 9 and 10, I'd get my ankles taped about six to eight inches above my ankle before the game. If you had very hairy legs, you had to put an underwrap on it. So the coaches would tell us to shave our legs from the upper ankles down. It made it easier. Now that's fine during basketball season but during the summer when you're wearing flip flops, people notice and want an explanation. I have two sisters, Jen and Angie. They've shaved their legs for years and didn't complain. So in grade 11, I started asking them questions about shaving cream and the best kind of razors. My sisters looked at me strangely, but I decided I didn't care what people would say, I'd shave my legs. I like the way it looks, the way it feels. I shave every other day. It makes me feel faster and cleaner. I also do it for style. If you're a guy in grade 8 or under, wait until you're in high school before even thinking about shaving your legs. And if you're under 16, ask your parents.

 Q once connected on 39 consecutive three-pointers during a training session.

Every day I shoot a round. When I start shooting and get a really good feeling in my arms, I call it "getting on fire." It's like being in the zone. They used to call this guy in the NBA the "Microwave" because it didn't take him long to heat up. I like to walk into a gym and start getting things heated up right away. The most I hit one time when I was on fire was 39 three-point shots. I don't normally get that many in a row. I shoot 85%. I usually hit seven or eight in a row before missing one. That personal record still stands today.

Q Mack

10   Q has a different hairstyle for every day of

Every day of the week, I pick something that is new and funky for my hair. Maybe one day I'll put my hair in "four corners." The four corners style is a plus sign on the top of my head. The sign is where my hair is parted. Another style is the braided afro. That consists of 25 to 30 little braids into a giant afro. Another one is the "unicorn" where I pull my hair back into an elastic on the top of my head. I wrap elastics around the hair into a unicorn point. I do double pony tails. I do spirals where my hair is split into 25 pieces in a grid. Instead of being in little braids, each one is in a spiral. I've got a couple friends who help me out with the more complicated hairdos. I feel I can pull off any look when I throw the energy and confidence behind it. You're having a bad hair day? So what. You can *always* have a good attitude day.